FACE OF DEATH

FACE OF DEATH

A Zoe Prime Mystery—Book 1

BLAKE PIERCE

BLAKE PIERCE

Debut author Blake Pierce is author of the ZOE PRIME MYSTERY series which includes FACE OF DEATH (Book #1), FACE OF MURDER (Book #2) and FACE OF FEAR (Book #3). Stella would love to hear from you, so please visit www.stellagoldauthor.com to receive free ebooks, hear the latest news, and stay in touch.

TABLE OF CONTENTS

PROLOGUE

Linda settled back in her chair, trying to get comfortable on the old, worn-out cushions. The seat, which had supported the weight of innumerable gas station attendants over the past fifteen or twenty years, was in about as good repair as the rest of the place.

At least she had a chair. And the TV, even if it was tiny and so out of date that she could only just make out faces through the noise on the screen.

Linda sighed and tapped the side of the TV a few times, trying to get a clearer picture. She was waiting for her favorite show to come on, and she wanted to at least be able to make out which character was which.

At least she wasn't likely to be disturbed. This corner of western Missouri was not exactly well frequented, and she could go hours between customers. No one lived for miles around, and the road had been supplanted by a new highway that took people to their destinations on a more direct route. It was probably only a matter of time before the place shut down, so Linda was enjoying her rest while she could get it.

The theme tune of her show came on, reassuringly familiar despite the tinny quality to the sound. Linda wriggled against the backrest again, trying to get as comfortable as possible, and helped herself to a bag of chips from the display behind her.

"Oh, Loretta," the character on the screen said. "How could you do this to me? Don't you know we're—"

The dialogue was drowned out by the bell above the door jingling. Linda shot to her feet, almost tripping over herself in an attempt to look as though she had been paying attention. Guiltily, she stuffed the open packet of chips on a shelf under the counter.

"Hi there," the customer said, smiling. He looked amused, but friendly, as if they were both sharing a private joke. "Uh, could I please use your restroom?"

He was pleasant enough. A skinny, boyish kind of man. He couldn't be thirty if he was a day. Linda liked him instantly. She had this kind of a sixth sense about customers. She could tell right away whether they were going to cause her any trouble.

"Sorry, hon," she said. "It's for paying customers only."

"Oh," he said, casting around him. There was a display of cheap candy by the side of the counter, designed to lure in kids who would tug at their parents' sleeves. "I'll take these."

He grabbed a bag of hard-shelled candy and tossed it gently onto the counter, right in front of her. He dug in his pocket for a handful of coins, and the correct change followed the bag.

"Here you are, sir," Linda said, sliding one of the bathroom keys across to him. "It's right at the back of the building. Just head outside and around the corner."

"Oh, thanks," the man said, taking it and tapping it against one thumb as he looked out to the parking lot. "But, uh. Would you mind showing me where it is?"

Linda hesitated. Her show was on, and she had missed so much of it already. And despite her feeling that this guy was perfectly good and normal—even handsome, if she was ten or fifteen years younger—she had a little niggling doubt in the back of her mind. Should she really abandon the counter to show him to the restroom? Go alone, in the dark, with a stranger, out of sight of the road?

Oh, Linda, she thought to herself. You're just trying to sneak some more time with your show. Now, you go on and get yourself up out of that chair and do your job.

"Sure," she said, though still somewhat reluctant. "Follow me."

The sun had gone down maybe half an hour ago, so it was really no wonder that he wanted a hand finding the bathroom. An

2

unfamiliar place in the dark wasn't easy to navigate. Linda began to lead him in the right direction, stepping over the weeds growing out of the concrete.

"This place sure is deserted, huh?" he said.

"Yeah," Linda said. Bit of an odd thing to bring up in the dark, wasn't it? Maybe he was feeling a little spooked himself, wanted some reassurance. Not that she enjoyed the isolation any more than he did. "We don't get a whole lot of traffic out here these days."

"I always think you can tell a whole lot about a place from its gas stations. There are these little signs, you know. Patterns you can pick up on. Like how rich a community is, or what kind of food is popular."

"I guess I never really thought of that." Privately, Linda could not care less about his explanation of the intricacies of gas stations across the country. She wanted to get out to the bathroom and get back inside as quickly as possible, with no weird stuff. But she didn't want to be rude and tell him that.

"Oh, yeah. I like visiting different ones. Some of them are huge, you know. Then some are little, beaten-up, out of the way places, like this one. And you can learn a lot about the people who work there, too."

That sent a prickle down Linda's spine. He was talking about her. She didn't want to ask what he could learn about her, or what he knew already. She didn't think she would like it.

"It's a strange job, out here in the middle of nowhere," he continued. "You must spend a lot of time alone. If you need help, well, it must be hard to get it. There's a certain type of person takes this kind of job. From there you can predict all kinds of things about behavior based on the patterns. Like how far you would be willing to go to serve a customer."

Linda quickened her steps across the dark ground, feeling the need to get away from him now. The reminder that she was vulnerable was not one she wanted to hear at that moment. It sent another shiver down her spine, even as she told herself she was being stupid.

She felt the hard metal of the front door key in her pocket, and slipped it between two of her fingers, where it could be a weapon.

She didn't say anything. She didn't want to trigger him into saying something else—or doing something. Though she couldn't say what she expected him to do, whatever it was, she was certain she didn't want it. They walked through the empty parking lot— the customer's car must have been parked around front at the pumps.

"There's your bathroom, over there," Linda said, pointing. She didn't particularly want to go any further. If he went on alone, she could get back to her counter, where there was a phone to call for help and doors she could lock.

The customer didn't say anything, but he pulled out his packet of candy and opened it up. He wasn't even looking at her, but seemed carefully concentrated on his task as he upended the packet and poured it all out.

The colorful balls of candy scattered and skipped across the concrete. Linda yelped and took a step back in spite of herself. Whoever heard of throwing candy all over the ground like that? Just to spook her, or what? Linda's hand flew to her chest, trying to calm her racing heartbeat.

"Look at that!" The customer laughed, pointing down at the candy. "It's always the same, you know? There's no such thing as randomness. You get the same patterns and fractals, and there's always something there. Even if you try not to see it, your head grabs onto a pattern, just like that."

Linda had heard enough. This guy was some kind of nutcase. She was alone out here, in the dark, as he had taken pains to point out. She had to get away from him, get back to the counter. Get back where it was safe.

Linda took the fastest route to that she could think of. She quickly marched the last few steps to the bathroom and unlocked it for him, the light above the door flickering on automatically.

"Oh!" the young man said. "There, look. On your hand. Another pattern."

Linda froze and looked down at her freckles, now visible in the pale orange light. His attention on her skin was like an insect, something she wanted instinctively to shake off.

"I have to get back in the store," Linda blurted out. "Just in case there are any more customers. Just leave the key when you're done."

She started hurrying back toward the front of the gas station, to the door and the safety of the counter. There was something off about this young man, something very odd indeed, and she did not want to spend another second in his company—even if it meant coming back for the key on her own later. All the hairs on the back of her neck were standing up, and her heart would not calm down.

Maybe she should call someone. She thought about her ex-husband, sitting miles away in his home, probably with his feet up in front of the TV. Or her boss, who for all she knew might have been in Canada for as often as she saw him. Would they even answer? And if they did, what could they do to help?

The police, maybe? No—surely that was an overreaction.

Linda almost tripped on a loose piece of candy that had skittered further than the rest, and tried to place her feet more carefully, checking the ground ahead. Her heart was racing, and she could hear her own footsteps crunching far too loudly as she rushed toward the corner of the building. She wished she could make less noise, go faster, just get back to the doors.

She was almost running, her breath catching in her chest. She turned the corner, feeling a sense of relief at seeing the familiar doors ahead.

But something was pulling her back—something tightening around her neck.

Linda's hands flew up instinctively, grasping at the thin, sharp wire that sliced at her fingers as she fought to get a purchase on it. Her feet tried aimlessly to move her body forward, the momentum only forcing her head further back. She had to get back to the doors. She had to get inside!

Panic clouded her vision, and the agonizing pressure intensified until there was a rush of release, something wet and hot gushing over her chest and down. There was no time to make sense of it all, only to gasp for air and feel a wet sucking sensation where the wire had been, and to notice the ground beneath her knees, and then her head, and then nothing at all.

CHAPTER ONE

FBI Special Agent Zoe Prime looked at the woman beside her in the passenger's seat and tried not to feel intimidated.

"How about getting thrown in at the deep end?" Shelley joked.

Zoe knew what she meant. The two of them had only just been partnered up, and here they were speeding toward a crime scene. A big crime scene, actually. One that would make serious headlines.

But that wasn't what was making Zoe feel uncomfortable. It was the fact that she had been partnered with a new agent who was already making waves at the Bureau. Shelley Rose had an open, kind face and manner, and was rumored to be able to get a confession out of anyone with just a smile. When you had a secret to hide, getting paired up with someone like that was more than enough to send a tickle of paranoia down your spine.

Not to mention the fact that Zoe, not considered the best at anything at the Bureau so far, was harboring a not-so-little amount of envy over the level of respect that her rookie partner already commanded.

Shelley had an almost-symmetrical face, just 1.5 millimeters off from being perfect, a slight variance between her eyes. There was no wonder she elicited automatic trust and amiability from those around her. It was classic psychology. A tiny flaw that made her beauty more human.

Even knowing that, Zoe couldn't help but find herself liking her new partner, too.

"What do we know so far?" Zoe asked.

Shelley leafed through the pile of papers she held in her hands, tucked inside a folder. "Convict busted out of Tent City, in Phoenix," she said. Outside the car, Arizona desert flashed by. "Fled on foot. Apparently, that hasn't slowed him down. Three known homicides so far."

"Guards?" Zoe asked. Her mind was flashing ahead. Counting the miles a man could get on foot in this heat. Not far, without rest, shelter, and water. Calculate for the sucking surface of the sand, and it reduced even further.

"No, randoms. Two hikers first." Shelley paused, sucking a breath in through her teeth. "The murders were…vicious, by all indications. Latest vic was a tourist on their way to the Grand Canyon."

"That is where we are headed now," Zoe assumed. The map of the area unfolded in her mind, carving out the roadways and paths each victim was likely to have taken in order to cross paths with their man.

"Right. Looks like we should brace ourselves."

Zoe nodded silently. She had noticed that it was harder for people like Shelley to turn up at a crime scene and see the victim's body. They felt the pain and suffering that had been inflicted. Zoe always just saw a body—meat. Meat that might hold clues that could help the investigation, and the numbers that circled around it.

That was probably what had allowed her to pass all the entrance exams and become a Special Agent in the first place—staying calm and controlled, analyzing the facts instead of the emotions. But it was her quiet nature and tendency to fall back on a blank facial expression that had left her in need of a new partner. Apparently, her last one had felt Zoe was too quiet and aloof.

She had attempted to remedy this on her first case with Shelley by purchasing two coffees in foam cups and supplying one to her partner when they met, in recognition of a seemingly ancient ritual between co-workers. It had seemed to go down well. Shelley was personable enough for the both of them, which was why Zoe was hopeful that this might actually work out.

It wasn't difficult to spot the site. Local cops milled around in uniform under the hot sun, a blazing ferocity that bore down heavily on her exposed arms as soon as Zoe stepped out of the air-conditioned car. Skin would burn in forty-five minutes if not protected. She would likely have some bronzing on her cheeks, nose, and hands by the time they got back into the car.

Shelley introduced them, and they both flashed their badges at the officer in charge before heading closer to the scene. Zoe only listened with half an ear, happy to let Shelley take charge. Even though Zoe was the superior officer, she did not begrudge Shelley throwing her weight around. Zoe was already searching, looking for the keys that would unlock everything for her. Shelley gave her a nod, an unspoken agreement that she would deal with the locals while Zoe examined the surroundings.

"I don't know as you'll find too much," the chief was saying. "We've been over everything about as closely as you can get."

Zoe ignored him and carried on looking. There were things that she could see, things that others couldn't. Things that might as well have been written in ten-foot-high letters, but were invisible to normal people.

This was her secret; her superpower. She spotted his footprints in the sand and the calculations appeared next to them, telling her everything she needed to know. It was as easy as reading a book.

She crouched slightly, getting a better look at the closest prints and how they stretched away from the victim's body. The perp was six foot two inches, his stride told her. The depth of his footprints easily indicated a weight around two-ten. He had been running steadily, approaching the victim at three point eight miles per hour to the attack, according to their spacing.

Zoe shifted over, examining the body next. The convict had used a seven-and-a-half-inch shiv, which he stabbed overhand into the body at a forty-nine-degree angle. Flight was in the northwest direction, at a faster jogging pace of five point nine miles per hour.

The blood in the sand told her it happened less than four hours ago. The calculations were easy. Using an average rate of fatigue and allowing for the heat of the day, Zoe looked up and squinted into the distance, picturing exactly how far away they would find him. Her heart quickened as she pictured bringing him in. They would catch him easily. Already fatigued, no water, and no way of knowing they had already discovered his crimes. This would be over soon.

Her attention strayed to the shrubs and small trees that grew across the distance, scattered growths that offered not enough shelter for a human. She saw the distances between them, numbers appearing before her eyes, telling her the story behind the pattern. Scattered far from each other, low natural resources. Clustered together, roots seeking out an underground water source and nutrient-rich ground. Even though they looked random to the unsuspecting eye, the placement of each was design. The design of the natural world.

"Anything?" Shelley asked. She had an expectant look, like she was waiting for her more experienced partner to solve everything.

Zoe looked up, starting guiltily. She rose to her feet and quickly shook her head. "Guess he ran that way," she said, pointing in the obvious direction of his receding footprints. There was an outcrop of rocks in the far distance, a good spot for a rest. The formation told her of wind patterns, of thousands of years of scooping and sculpting. "Maybe he will stop for shade over there. It is a hot day."

A secret was a secret. There was no way she could admit to what she knew. No way that she could say out loud that she was a freak who understood the world in a way that no one else did. Or admit the rest—that she didn't get how they saw it, either. But she could give them this much. The kind of hint that a normal person might see.

The chief cleared his throat, interrupting. "We already scouted in that direction and found nothing. The dogs lost the scent. There's some rockier ground over there which doesn't take footprints. We figure he would have carried on running straight ahead. Or even been picked up by a vehicle."

Zoe narrowed her eyes. She knew what she knew. This man was running in desperation, his stride long, body low to the ground as he pitched forward for speed. He wasn't heading to a rescue, and he wasn't so far away they wouldn't be able to find him.

"Humor us," Zoe suggested. She tapped the FBI sigil on her badge, still held in her hand. There was one great thing about being a special agent: you weren't always expected to explain yourself. In fact, you played into stereotypes if you didn't.

Shelley turned back from studying Zoe's face to liaise with the chief again, an air of determination about her. "Send up the chopper. You have the dogs ready?"

"Sure." The chief nodded, though he looked none too pleased. "You're the boss."

Shelley thanked him. "Let's drive out," she suggested to Zoe. "I have the pilot on the radio. He'll keep us updated when they spot anything."

Zoe nodded and got back into the car obediently. Shelley had supported her, backed her up. That was a good sign. She was grateful, and had no sense of ego at Shelley being the one to give the orders. It was all the same, so long as lives got saved.

"Whew." Shelley paused, resting in the passenger's seat with a map open in her hands. "Doesn't get any easier, does it? A woman on her own like that, no provocation. She didn't deserve that."

Zoe nodded again. "Right," she said, not sure of what else she could add to the conversation. She started the car and began driving, to fill the space.

"You don't talk a whole lot, do you?" Shelley asked. She paused before adding, "It's all right. Just getting to know how you work."

The murder was undeserved, that was true. Zoe could see and understand that. But what was done, was done. They had a job to do now. Seconds ticked on, beyond the normal limitations of an expected reply. Zoe cast about but could find nothing to say. The time had passed. If she spoke up now, she would only sound stranger still.

Zoe tried to focus on holding a sad expression while she drove, but it was too difficult to do both at once. She stopped struggling to do it, her face relaxing into her natural blank stare. It wasn't that she wasn't thinking, or that there were no emotions at all behind her eyes. It was just difficult to think about how her face looked and consciously control it, while her mind calculated the exact distance between each marker on the road and ensured she stayed at a speed which would prevent the car from flipping if she had to swerve on this type of tarmac.

They took the road, following the smoother surface as it curved around through the flat landscape. Zoe could already see that it would move the right way, allowing them to catch up with him if he ran in a straight line. She put her foot down hard on the pedal, using the advantage of tarmac to speed onward.

A voice crackled over the radio, breaking Zoe out of her inner thoughts.

"We've got eyes on the suspect. Over."

"Roger that," Shelley replied. She was precise and wasted no time, which Zoe appreciated. "Coordinates?"

The helicopter pilot rattled off his position, and Shelley directed Zoe from her map. They didn't have to adjust their course—they were right on target. Zoe clenched the wheel tighter, feeling that thrill of validation. She'd been correct with her assumptions.

It was only a few moments more before they sighted the chopper hanging steadily in the air above a local patrol car, whose two occupants had apparently gotten out and tackled the convict to the ground. He lay in the sand, newly disturbed and shifting around him, and swore.

Zoe pulled the car to a stop and Shelley hopped out immediately, relaying information over her handheld radio. A small group of men with dogs were already approaching from the southeast, the dogs barking in excitement at finding the source of the scent they had picked up.

Zoe picked up the map that Shelley had discarded, checking it against the GPS. They were within an eighth of a mile of where she had guessed he would be, on a direct trajectory. He must have run from the outcropping when he heard the dogs.

She allowed herself a victory smile, jumping out of the car to join them with renewed vigor. Out under the burning sun, Shelley flashed her a matching grin, obviously happy to be closing their first case together already.

Later, back in the car, the quiet settled in again. Zoe didn't know what to say—she never did. Small talk was an absolute mystery to her. What was the correct number of times to mention the weather before it became an obvious cliché? For how many drives could she engage in dry conversation about things that didn't really matter before the silence became companionable, rather than awkward?

"You didn't say much out there," Shelley said, breaking the silence at last.

Zoe paused before answering. "No," she agreed, trying to make it sound friendly. There wasn't much more that she could do beyond agreeing.

There was more silence. Zoe calculated the seconds inside her head, realizing it had gone beyond what would be considered a normal break in conversation.

Shelley cleared her throat. "The partners I had in training, we practiced talking through the case," she said. "Work together to solve it. Not alone."

Zoe nodded, keeping her eyes fixed ahead on the road. "I understand," she said, even though she felt a rising sense of panic. She didn't understand—not fully. On some level she understood the way people felt around her, because they were always telling her. But she didn't know what she was supposed to do about it. She was already trying, trying as hard as she could.

"Talk to me next time," Shelley said, settling deeper into her seat as if it was all resolved. "We're supposed to be partners. I want to really work together."

This didn't bode well for the future. Zoe's last partner had taken at least a few weeks to work himself up to complaining about how quiet and aloof she was.

She had thought she was doing better this time. Hadn't she bought the coffees? And Shelley had smiled at her before. Was she supposed to buy more drinks, to tip the balance? Was there a certain number she should aim for in order to make their relationship more comfortable?

Zoe watched the road flash in front of the windshield, under a sky that was starting to darken. She felt like she should say something else, though she couldn't imagine what. This was all her fault, and she knew it.

It always seemed so easy for other people. They talked, and talked, and talked, and became friends overnight. She had observed it happening so many times, but there didn't seem to be any rules to follow. It wasn't defined by a set period of time or number of interactions, or the amount of things people needed to have in common.

They were just magically good at getting on with other people, like Shelley was. Or they weren't. Like Zoe.

Not that she knew what she was doing wrong. People told her to be warmer and more friendly, but what did that mean, exactly? No one had ever given her a manual explaining all of the things she was supposed to know. Zoe gripped the steering wheel tighter, trying not to betray how upset she felt. That was the last thing she needed Shelley to see.

Zoe realized that it was she herself who was the problem. She wasn't delusional about that. She just didn't know how to be any way other than what she was, and other people did, and she was embarrassed that she had never learned. To admit that would be, somehow, even worse.

The plane journey home was even more awkward.

Shelley flipped casually through the pages of a women's magazine that had been on sale in the airport, giving each page no more than a cursory glance before she gave up and moved on. After finishing it cover to cover, she glanced at Zoe; then, seeming to think better of starting up a conversation, she opened the magazine again, spending more time on the articles.

Zoe hated reading things like that. The pictures, the words, everything jumping out at her from the page. Clashing font sizes and faces, contradictory articles. Images purporting to prove a celebrity had plastic surgery, showing only the normal variance for changes in the face over time and with age, calculable easily to anyone with a basic grasp of human biology.

Multiple times, Zoe tried to force herself to think of something to say to her new partner. She couldn't talk about the magazine. What else might they have in common? The words wouldn't come.

"Good solve on our first case," she said at last, murmuring it, almost not brave enough to say even that.

Shelley looked up in surprise, her eyes wide and blank for a moment before she lapsed into a grin. "Oh, yeah," she said. "We did good."

"Hopefully the next one will be just as smooth." Zoe felt her insides shriveling. Why was she so bad at small talk? It was taking every ounce of concentration to find the next line to say.

"Maybe we can make it quicker next time," Shelley suggested. "You know, when we're really in tune with each other, we'll be working much faster."

Zoe felt that like a blow. They could have caught the guy quicker, gotten the helicopter above his precise location from the moment they arrived, if Zoe had just shared what she knew. If she hadn't been so cautious about how she knew it that she kept it hidden.

"Maybe," she said, noncommittal. She tried to direct a smile Shelley's way that might be reassuring, from a more experienced agent to a rookie. Shelley returned it with a little hesitation, and went back to her magazine.

They didn't speak again until they landed.

CHAPTER TWO

Zoe pushed open the door to her apartment with a sigh of relief. Here was her haven, the place where she could relax and stop trying to be the person that everyone else accepted.

There was a soft mewling from the direction of the kitchen as she switched on the lights, and Zoe headed straight over there after depositing her keys on the side table.

"Hi, Euler," she said, bending down to scratch one of her cats behind the ears. "Where is Pythagoras?"

Euler, a gray tabby, only mewled again in response, looking across to the cupboard where Zoe kept the bags and cans of cat food.

Zoe didn't need a translator to understand that. Cats were simple enough. The only interaction they really craved was food and the occasional scratch.

She took a new can out of the cupboard and opened it, spooning it into a food bowl. Her Burmese, Pythagoras, soon caught the scent and padded over from some other part of their home.

Zoe watched them eat for a moment, wondering if they wished they had another human to look after them. Living alone meant that they were fed when she got home, no matter what time that might turn out to be. Doubtless, they would have appreciated a more regular schedule—but there were always the neighborhood mice to track down if they got hungry. And looking at them now, Pythagoras had put on a couple of pounds lately. He could do to diet.

It wasn't as if Zoe was about to get married anyway—for the cats or for any other reason. She'd never even had a properly serious relationship. After the upbringing she'd had, she had almost resigned herself to the fact that she was destined to die alone.

Her mother had been strictly religious, and that meant intolerant. Zoe had never been able to find anywhere in the Bible where it said you had to communicate like everyone else and think in linguistic riddles instead of mathematical formulae, but her mother had read it there all the same. She had been convinced that something was wrong with her daughter, something sinful.

Zoe's hand strayed to her collarbone, traced the line where a silver crucifix had once hung on a silver chain. For many long years of her childhood and adolescence, she hadn't been able to take the thing off without being accused of blasphemy—not even to shower or sleep.

Not that there had been much she could do, without getting accused of being the devil's child.

"Zoe," her mother would say, shaking a finger and pursing her lips. "You just quit that demon logic now. The devil is in you, child. You've got to cast him right out."

Demon logic, apparently, was mathematics, especially when present in a child of six years old.

Over and over again, her mother would bring up how different she was. When Zoe didn't socialize with the children her own age in kindergarten, or school. When she didn't take up any after-school clubs except for extra study in math and science, and even then didn't form groups or make friends. When she understood ratios in cooking after watching her mother bake things just once.

Very quickly, Zoe had learned to suppress her natural instinct for numbers. When she knew the answers to the questions people asked without having to even work them out, she kept quiet. When she figured out which of the kids in her class had stolen the teacher's keys and hidden them, and where they must have been hidden, all through proximity and the clues left behind, she didn't say a word.

In many ways, not much had changed since that scared little six-year-old, desperate to please her mother, had stopped saying every little weird thing that came into her mind and started pretending to be normal.

Zoe shook her head, bringing her attention back to the present. That was more than twenty-five years ago. No use dwelling on it now.

She glanced out of her window at the Bethesda skyline, looking as she always did in the precise direction of Washington, DC. She had figured out the right way to look the day she had signed the lease, noting several local landmarks which lined up to show her a compass direction. It wasn't anything political or patriotic; she just liked the way they matched up, creating that perfect line on the map.

It was dark out, and even the lights of the other buildings around hers were being extinguished, one by one. It was late; late enough that she should be getting on with things and going to bed.

Zoe fired up her laptop and quickly tapped in her password, opening her email inbox to check for any updates. The last task of her day. There were a few she could quickly delete—junk mail, mostly messages about sales for brands she had never shopped for and scams from supposed Nigerian princes.

Clearing the junk left her with a few more she could read and then discard, missives that needed no reply. Updates from social media, which she rarely visited, and newsletters from websites that she followed.

One was a little more interesting. A ping through from her online dating profile. A short but sweet message—some guy asking for a date. Zoe clicked through to his page and examined his images, considering them. She quickly assessed his actual height, and was pleasantly surprised to find that it matched up with what he had written in his details. Maybe someone with a little honesty about him.

The next was yet more intriguing, but even so, Zoe felt an urge to put off reading it. It was from her mentor and former professor, Dr. Francesca Applewhite. She could predict what the doctor was going to ask before she read it, and she wasn't going to like it.

Zoe sighed and opened it anyway, resigned to the need to get it over with. Dr. Applewhite was brilliant, the kind of mathematician she had always dreamed of being until she realized she could put her talents to use as an agent. Francesca was also the only other person who knew the truth about the way her mind worked—the synesthesia that turned clues into visual numbers into facts in her head. The only person she liked and trusted enough to talk about it with.

Actually, Dr. Applewhite had been the one to turn her on to the FBI in the first place. She owed her a lot. But that wasn't why she was reluctant to read her message.

Hi Zoe, the email read. *Just wanted to ask whether you've contacted the therapist I suggested. Have you been able to schedule a session? Let me know if you need any help.*

Zoe sighed. She had not contacted the therapist, and she didn't truly know whether she was going to. She closed the email without replying, relegating it to one of tomorrow's problems.

Euler jumped up onto her lap, obviously having satisfied himself with his dinner, and started to purr. Zoe gave him another scratch, looking at her screen, deciding.

Pythagoras let out an indignant mew at being neglected, and Zoe glanced at him with an affectionate smile. It wasn't exactly a sign, but it was enough to push her into action. She went back to the previous message, from the dating site, and typed out a response before she could change her mind.

Would love to meet. When is good for you?—Z.

"After you," he said, smiling and gesturing toward the breadbasket.

Zoe smiled back and picked up a piece of bread, her mind automatically calculating the width and depth of each piece to pick one that was somewhere in the middle range. Didn't want to look too greedy now.

"So, what do you do, John?" Zoe asked. It was easy enough to get the conversation started this way—she had been on enough dates to know that it was standard form. Besides that, it was always a good idea to make sure that he had a good income.

"I'm a lawyer," John said, taking his own serving of bread. Biggest piece. Somewhere in the region of 300 calories. He would be halfway to full before their main course came. "I mostly deal with property disputes, so there's not much overlap between your work and mine."

Zoe noted the average salary for a property lawyer in their area and nodded mutely, calculations flashing through her mind. Between them they would probably be well set for a mortgage on a three-bedroom property, and that was just for starters. Room for a nursery. Enough career scope to upgrade later on down the line.

His face was almost symmetrical, too. Funny how that was coming up lately. There was just one twist, a certain way he had of smiling that lifted up his right cheek while the left stayed more or less in position. A lopsided smile. There was something charming about it, perhaps because of the asymmetry. She counted the correct number of perfectly straight, white teeth flashing between his lips.

"So, how about your family? Any siblings?" John tried, his tone faltering a little.

Zoe realized she had been expected to at least make some kind of comment on his work, and picked herself up mentally. "Just me," she said. "I was raised by my mom. We are not close."

John lifted an eyebrow for the barest second before nodding. "Oh, that sucks. My family is pretty tight. We get together for family meals at least once a month."

Zoe's eyes flicked over his lean physique, and she decided that he must not have been eating too badly at those dinners. Mind you, he clearly went to the gym. What could he bench? Maybe 200 pounds, judging by those arm muscles rippling under his blue striped shirt.

There had been silence between them for a few moments now. Zoe ripped off a piece of bread and shoved it into her mouth, then chewed it as fast as she could to free her mouth again. People didn't speak while they ate, at least not in polite society, so that served as kind of an excuse, as far as she was concerned.

"Is it just you and your parents?" Zoe asked, as soon as the bite had sunk down her throat, thick and clinging. *No,* she thought. *Two siblings, at least.*

"I have an older brother and sister," John said. "There's only four years between us, so we get along pretty well."

Behind him, over his shoulder, Zoe saw their five-foot-three waitress struggling with a heavy tray of drinks. Two bottles of wine split amongst seven glasses, all destined for a rowdy table at the end of a line of booths. All the same age. College friends, having a reunion.

"That must be nice," Zoe said distantly. She didn't think it would have been nice, really, to have older siblings. She didn't have a clue at all about what it must have been like. It was just a different experience that she had never had.

"I'd say so."

John's responses were getting more distant. He wasn't asking her questions anymore. They hadn't even gotten through to the main course yet.

It was with some relief that Zoe saw the waitress bringing over two plates, balanced expertly on her arm, the weight distributed evenly between elbow and palm.

"Oh, our food is here," she said, just to distract him more than anything else.

John looked around, moving with a lithe grace which certainly underscored his commitment to the gym. He was a good enough man. Handsome, charming, with a good job. Zoe tried to focus on him, to apply herself. When eating it should be easier. She stared at the food on her plate—*twenty-seven peas, exactly two inches thick on the steak*—and tried not to let anything distract her from what he was saying.

Still, she heard the awkward silences just as much as he did.

At the end, he offered to pay for everything— *$37.97 her fair share*—and Zoe gratefully accepted. She forgot that she was supposed to argue at least once, to give him the chance to insist, but she remembered it when she saw the slight downturn at the corners of his mouth as he offered his credit card to the waitress.

"Well, it's been a great night," John said, looking around and buttoning up his suit jacket as he stood. "This is a lovely restaurant."

"The food was wonderful," Zoe murmured, getting up even though she would have preferred to sit for longer.

"It was nice to meet you, Zoe," he said. He offered her his hand to shake. When she took it, he leaned in and kissed her on the cheek, as briefly as possible, before moving away again.

No offer to walk her to her car, or drive her home. No hug, no request to see her again. John was pleasant enough—all lopsided smile and careful gestures—but the message was clear.

"You too, John," Zoe said, allowing him to walk out of the restaurant ahead of her while she gathered her purse, so that there would be no awkward small talk on the journey to the parking lot.

In the privacy of her car, Zoe slumped into the driver's seat and buried her head in her hands. Stupid, stupid, stupid. Imagine being so preoccupied with the stride length of the various members of the wait staff that you can't even focus on your charming, handsome, extremely eligible date.

Things were going too far. Zoe knew it, in her heart of hearts, and had maybe known it for a while. She was getting so she could barely concentrate on social cues at all without getting her head turned by calculations and exploration of patterns. It was bad enough that she didn't understand all of the cues when she heard or saw them, but not to notice them at all was even worse.

"What a freak," she muttered to herself, knowing she was the only person who would hear it. That made her want to laugh and cry at the same time.

The whole drive home, Zoe tossed and turned the events of the evening through her mind. Seventeen awkward pauses. Twenty occasions, at least, when John must have wanted her to show more interest. Who knew how many that she didn't even notice. One free steak dinner—not enough to make up for feeling like the kind of outcast who was going to die alone and lonely.

With cats, of course.

Not even Euler and Pythagoras, mewling and attempting to rival one another for the right to jump into her lap on the sofa, could make her feel better. She scooped them both up and settled them down, not at all surprised when they both immediately lost interest and started prowling along the back of the sofa.

She opened the email from Dr. Applewhite one more time, looking at the number she had sent her for the therapist.

It couldn't hurt, could it?

Zoe entered the number into her cell one digit at a time, even though she had memorized it at a glance. She felt her breath catch as her finger hovered above the green call button, but forced it down anyway, the cell up to her ear.

Ring-ring-ring.

Ring-ring-ring.

"Hello," said a female voice on the other end of the line.

"Hello—" Zoe started, but cut herself off immediately as the voice continued.

"You have reached the offices of Dr. Lauren Monk. Apologies, but we are currently out of office hours."

Zoe groaned internally. Voicemail.

"If you would like to book an appointment, change an arranged appointment, or leave a message, please do so after the t—"

Zoe yanked the cell away from her ear as if it was on fire, and cancelled the call. Into the silence, Pythagoras mewed heartily, then jumped from the arm of the sofa up onto her shoulder.

She was going to have to make the appointment, and she was going to have to do it soon. She promised herself that. But it wouldn't hurt to leave it one more day, would it?

CHAPTER THREE

"**Y**ou'll burn in hell," her mother announced. She had a triumphant look on her face, a kind of madness lighting up her eyes. Looking closer, Zoe realized it was the reflection of flames. "Devil child, you'll burn in hell for all eternity!"

The heat was unbearable. Zoe struggled to get to her feet, to move, but something was tying her down. Her legs were like lead, anchored down to the floor, and she could not lift them. She could not get away.

"Mom!" Zoe cried out. "Mom, please! It is getting hotter—it hurts!"

"You'll burn forever," her mother cackled, and in front of Zoe's eyes, her skin turned red as an apple, horns growing from the top of her head and a tail sprouting behind her. "You'll burn, daughter mine!"

The shrill ring of her cell woke Zoe from her dream with a start, and Pythagoras opened one baleful green eye on her before scrambling off his position on top of her ankles and stalking away.

Zoe shook her head, trying to get her bearings. Right. She was in her own bedroom in Bethesda, and her cell was ringing.

Zoe fumbled with the device to accept the call, her fingers slow and thick from sleep. "Hello?"

"Special Agent Prime, I apologize for the late hour," her boss said.

Zoe glanced at the clock. Just after three in the morning. "That is okay," she said, dragging herself to a sitting position. "What is it?"

"We've got a case in the Midwest which could use your help. I know you just got home—we can send someone else if it's too much."

"No, no," Zoe said hastily. "I can take it."

24

The work would do her some good. Feeling useful and solving cases was the only thing that made her feel like she might have something in common with her fellow humans. After last night's debacle, it would be a welcome relief to throw herself into something new.

"All right. I'll get you and your partner on a plane in a couple of hours. You're going to Missouri."

A little south of Kansas City, the rental car rolled up outside a little station and came to a stop.

"This is it," Shelley said, consulting the GPS one last time.

"Finally," Zoe sighed, relinquishing her tight grip on the steering wheel and rubbing her eyes. The flight had been a red-eye, chasing the sun as it rose across the sky. It was still early morning, and she already felt like she had been awake for a whole day. A lack of sleep followed directly by a rush to catch a plane could do that to you.

"I need some coffee," Shelley said, before jumping out.

Zoe was inclined to agree. The flight, brief as it was, had been interruption after interruption. The rise into the air, stewardesses offering breakfast and juices no fewer than five times, and then the descent—no time to snatch a little more sleep. Even though the two of them had spent most of the journey in silence, discussing only their plans for landing and where they would get the rental car, they had not gained any extra rest.

Zoe trailed after Shelley into the building, once again belying her role as the superior and more experienced agent. Shelley might have received more praise, but Zoe was no green rookie. She had more than enough cases under her belt, the days of her training faded so far into the distance that she barely remembered them. Still, it felt more comfortable to follow.

Shelley introduced herself to the local sheriff, and he nodded and shook hands with both of them when Zoe parroted her own name.

"Glad to see you folks coming in," he said. That was something of note. Usually the locals were resentful, feeling that they could take care of the case themselves. It was only when they knew they were out of their depth that they were glad of the help.

"Hopefully, we can get this tied up nicely and be out of your hair by the end of the day," Shelley said, throwing an easy grin at Zoe. "Special Agent Prime here is on a roll. We got our first case together closed in a matter of hours, didn't we, Z?"

"Three hours and forty-seven minutes," Zoe replied, including the time that it had taken to get their escaped convict through processing.

She wondered briefly about how Shelley could give her that open, easy smile. It looked genuine enough, but then Zoe never had been good at telling the difference—not unless there was some kind of tic or sign in the face, a crease around the eyes at the right angle to indicate that something was off. After their last case, not to mention the almost silent plane and car ride here, she had expected there to be some tension between them.

The sheriff inclined his head. "Would be mighty good to get you on a plane back home by nightfall, if you don't mind me saying so. Would mean a weight off my shoulders."

Shelley laughed. "Don't worry. We're the guys you never want to see, right?"

"No offense meant," the sheriff cheerily agreed. He weighed one hundred and eighty-five pounds, Zoe thought, watching him walk with that particular wide-foot angle that was common to the overweight.

They moved into his office and started going over the briefing. Zoe picked up the files and started leafing through.

"Hit me with it, Z," Shelley said, leaning back in her chair and waiting expectantly.

It seemed like she had a nickname already.

Zoe looked up with some surprise, but seeing that Shelley was serious, she began to read aloud. "Three bodies in three days, it looks like. The first one was in Nebraska, the second in Kansas, and the third in Missouri—here."

"What, is our perp going on a road trip?" Shelley scoffed.

Zoe marked the lines in her head, drawing a connection between the towns. A mostly southeastern direction; the most likely continued course was down through the rest of Missouri to Arkansas, Mississippi, maybe a bit of Tennessee down near Memphis. Presuming, of course, that they didn't stop him first.

"The latest murder occurred outside of a gas station. The lone attendant was the victim. Her body was found outside."

Zoe could picture it in her head. A dark and lonely gas station, a postcard picture of any other lonesome gas station in this part of the country. Isolated, the lights above the parking lot the only ones for miles around. She started to rifle through the photographs of the scene, handing them over to Shelley when she was done.

A firmer picture was emerging. A woman left dead on the ground, facing back toward the entrance—returning from somewhere. Was she lured outside and then attacked as she let her guard down? Some kind of noise she could pass off as coyotes, or maybe a customer complaining of car trouble?

Whatever it was, it was enough to lure her outside into the dark, at night, in the cold air—away from her post. It had to have been something.

"All female victims," Zoe continued reading. "No particular match in their appearance. Different age groups, hair color, weight, height. Their only thing in common is their gender."

As she spoke, Zoe pictured the women in her head, standing up against a mugshot board. One five foot four, one five foot seven, one five foot ten. Quite a difference. Three inches each time—was that a clue? No; they were killed out of order. The short woman was the heaviest, the taller one light and therefore thin. Probably easier to overwhelm physically, despite her size.

Different altitudes. Different distances from crime scene to crime scene—no hint of a formula or algorithm that would tell her how far away the next one would be. Topography at the murder sites was different.

"They look ... random."

Shelley sighed, shaking her head. "I was afraid you would say that. What about the motive?"

"Crime of opportunity, maybe. Each woman was murdered at night, in an isolated place. There were no witnesses and no CCTV cameras turned on at any of the sites. The CSIs say there was hardly anything left behind in the way of evidence at all."

"So, we have a psycho with a need for murder, who has just now decided to go on a rampage, and yet has enough control to keep himself safe," Shelley summarized. Her tone was dry enough that Zoe could tell she was feeling just as uneasy as Zoe herself.

This wasn't going to be the easy, open-and-shut case she had been hoping for.

CHAPTER FOUR

The gas station was eerily quiet when Zoe pulled up, alone, at the crime scene. There was tape everywhere, holding off would-be spectators, and a single officer stationed at the front door to keep watch for rebellious teenagers.

"Morning," Zoe said, flashing her badge. "I am going to take a look around."

The man nodded his consent, not that she required it, and she passed him, ducking under the tape to head inside.

Shelley had known the best way to deploy their unique and particular skills. Without prior discussion, she had suggested that she would go and interview the family, dispatching Zoe to the scene of the latest murder after a drop-off at the home. That was only right. Zoe could find the patterns here, and Shelley would know how to read emotions and lies there. Zoe had to give her that.

So, she had agreed, and given only the pretense of being in charge. It was only Shelley's warm nature—and Zoe's overall lack of care for the command structure's correct adherence, so long as the case was solved—that made it feel all right. Shelley had even seemed almost apologetic, so keen to show that she knew the ropes that she was overstepping her bounds by accident.

She hesitated at the door of the gas station, knowing things must have started there. There were faint marks left on the ground, footprints marked by small flags and plastic triangles. The woman—the older woman with sensible shoes and a short stride—had led the way. This gas station was so isolated that she couldn't have had more than a few customers that day, and the marks were clear of any confusion only a few paces away from the door.

The woman had been followed, though perhaps she had not known it. The numbers appeared before Zoe's eyes, telling her everything she needed to know: the distance between them indicated an unhurried stride. There were no other footsteps to indicate whether the perpetrator had come from inside the gas station or somewhere in the parking lot. The woman had walked calmly, at a steady pace, toward the corner. There was a mess here, but Zoe passed it, seeing the steps continuing and knowing she would be back again eventually.

First, the footsteps continued at a slightly faster pace. Was the woman aware now that she was followed?

Here—right by a few scattered pieces of candy that littered the ground, perhaps from a botched delivery or a clumsy child—they had stopped. The woman had turned to look at the man, before spinning on her heel and rushing onward toward a door at the back of the building.

There was a key still hanging from the lock, swinging slightly every now and then in the breeze. The ground was slightly scuffed here, where the victim had stopped to turn it in the lock and then hurried away.

Her retreating steps showed a much longer stride, a quicker pace. She had been almost running, trying to get away and back to the store she tended. Was she afraid? Cold in the dark? Just wanting to get back to her desk?

The man had followed her. Not immediately; there was an indentation here, a scuff of raised dirt at the edge of a heel print where he had slowly turned to watch her. Then he had loped after her with what was likely an easy, light gait, directly approaching her, cutting inside her path to reach her at the corner.

Ah, the mess again. Zoe squatted on her heels, examining it closer. The ground was more profoundly disturbed here, scuff marks clearly visible where the victim had kicked for purchase for perhaps a few seconds or less. More noticeable was the heavier imprint of the man's shoes here, where he must have taken some of her weight on the garrote.

The body had already been taken away, but the blood spoke for itself.

It must have been fast; she would not have struggled for long.

Zoe peered down for a closer look at the footprints she had seen, those of the male culprit. What was interesting was their appearance. While she could make out a faint pattern in the marks left by the victim—enough to give an idea of brand and the comfortable style of shoe—his footprints were a vague outline only, an impression of a heel for the most part.

Zoe retraced her steps, checking as she went. There were only two places where she could make out his steps: near the door, where he had waited, and here, at the moment of death. In both cases, all identifying marks—including the length and width of the shoe—had been erased.

In other words, he had cleaned up after himself.

"There was no physical evidence left other than the body?" Zoe asked the guard, who had not yet moved from his position by the door.

He had his thumbs hooked in his belt loops, his eyes squinting up and down the road in either direction. "No, ma'am," he said.

"No hair follicles? Tire tracks?"

"Nothing that we can pinpoint to a perpetrator. Looks like all of the tire tracks in the parking lot were erased, not just his."

Zoe chewed her lip, thinking. He might have been choosing his victims at random, but he was far from being a crazed madman. Just like Shelley had said—he was in control. More than that, he was patient and meticulous. Even killers who planned their attacks weren't usually this good.

Zoe's ringtone blazed out across the quiet of the empty road, making the guard jump in his boots. "Special Agent Prime," she answered automatically, without even checking the caller display.

"Z, I've got a lead. Abusive ex-husband," Shelley said. No standing on ceremony for her. Her tone was rushed, excited. That thrill of the first hint. "Looks like the divorce was just being finalized. You want to come pick me up and check it out?"

"Not much to see here," Zoe replied. There was no sense in both of them walking the scene, if there were other leads to be followed. Besides, she got the feeling that Shelley very much did not want to see the place where a woman had lost her life. She was still a little green in many ways. "I will be with you in twenty minutes."

"So, where were you last night?" Shelley pressed, leaning in to make the guy feel as though it was their little secret.

"I was at a bar," he grunted. "Lucky's, over on the east side of town."

Zoe was listening, but only just. She had known from the moment they walked in that this was not their murderer. The ex-husband might have liked to throw his weight around when they were married, but that was exactly the problem: his weight. He was at least a hundred pounds too heavy to have left those imprints, and too short, besides. He had the height to take out his wife—a smaller woman who had no doubt been subjected to his fists many times over—but not the tallest victim. He was five foot seven, six and three-quarters at a better guess. It would have been too much of a reach.

"Can anyone verify you were there?" Shelley asked.

Zoe wanted to stop her, prevent any more wasted time. But she didn't say a thing. She didn't want to try to explain something that was as obvious to her as the sky being blue.

"I was passed out," he said, throwing his hand in the air in a gesture of frustration. "Check the cameras. Ask the bartender. He kicked me out well after midnight."

"The bartender has a name?" Zoe asked, flipping out a pad to make a note. At least it would be something they could easily verify. She noted down what he told her.

"When did you last see your ex-wife?" Shelley asked.

He shrugged, his eyes moving sideways as he thought. "I don't know. Bitch was always getting in my way. Guess a few months ago. She was getting all het up about alimony. I missed a few payments."

Shelley visibly bristled at the way he spoke. There were some emotions that Zoe found hard to read, elusive things that didn't quite have names or that came from sources she couldn't identify with. But anger was easy. Anger might as well have been a red flashing sign, and it was going off over Shelley's head at that moment.

"Do you consider all women to be inconveniences, or just the ones who divorced you after a violent assault?"

The man's eyes practically bulged out of his head. "Hey, look, you can't—"

Shelley interrupted him before he could finish. "You have a history of harming Linda, don't you? We have several arrests for various domestic violence complaints on your record. Seems you made a habit of beating her black and blue."

"I…" The man shook his head, as if trying to clear it. "I never hurt her like that. Like, bad. I wouldn't kill her."

"Why not? Surely you'd want to be rid of those alimony payments?" Shelley pressed.

Zoe tensed, her hands making fists. Any longer, and she was going to have to intervene. Shelley was getting carried away, her voice rising in pitch and volume at the same time.

"I ain't been paying them anyway," he pointed out. His arms were crossed defensively over his chest.

"So, maybe you just saw red one last time, is that it? You wanted to hurt her, and it went further than ever before?"

"Stop it!" he yelled out, his composure breaking. He put his hands over his face unexpectedly, then dropped them to reveal moisture smeared from his eyes down his cheeks. "I stopped paying the alimony so she would come see me. I missed her, all right? Stupid bitch had a hold on me. I go out and get drunk every night 'cause I'm all alone. Is that what you want to hear? Is it?"

They were done—that much was clear. Still, Shelley thanked the man stiffly and handed over a card, asking him to give them a call if anything else came to mind. The things that Zoe might have done, if she had thought it would do any good. Most people didn't call Zoe back.

On this occasion, she very much doubted that Shelley would get a call either.

Shelley blew out a heavy breath as they were walking away. "Dead end. Sorry, no pun intended. I buy his story. What are you thinking we should do next?"

"I would like to see the body," Zoe replied. "If there are any more clues to be found, they are with the victim."

CHAPTER FIVE

The coroner's office was a squat building beside the precinct, along with just about everything else in this tiny town. There was just one road that swept right through, stores and a small elementary school and everything a town needed to survive placed either to the left or the right.

It made Zoe uncomfortable. Too much like home.

The coroner was waiting for them downstairs, the victim already laid out on the table for them like a grisly presentation. The man, an older fellow just a few years from retirement with a certain amount of waffle and bumble about him, began a long and winding explanation of his findings, but Zoe filtered him out.

She could see the things he would tell them laid out before her. The slash wound at the neck told her the precise gauge of wire they were looking for. The woman weighed just over 170 pounds despite her smaller stature, though a fair amount of that had gushed out of her along with almost three liters of her blood.

The angle of the incision and the force applied to it told her two things. First, that the killer was between five foot ten and six foot nothing. Secondly, that he was not relying on strength to commit the crimes. The victim's weight did not hang on the wire for long. When she collapsed, he let her go down. That, combined with the choice of wire as a weapon in the first place, likely meant that he was not very strong.

Not very strong combined with tall enough likely meant that he was neither muscular nor heavy. If he had been either, his own body weight would have served as a counterbalance. That meant he likely had a slim build, quite in line with what one would normally picture when thinking of an average man, of average height.

There was only one thing that she could say for certain was not average, and that was his act of murder.

As for the rest, there was nothing much to go on. His hair color, his name, what city he came from, why he was doing this—none of that was written in the empty and abandoned shell of the thing that used to be a woman in front of them.

"So, what we can tell from this," the coroner was saying slowly, his voice querulous and long-winded. "Is that the killer was likely of an average male height, perhaps between five feet nine and just above six feet tall."

Zoe only just restrained herself from shaking her head. That was far too wide an estimate.

"Has the victim's family been in touch?" Shelley asked.

"Nothing since the ex-husband came to identify." The coroner shrugged.

Shelley clasped a small pendant at her throat, tugging it back and forward on a slim gold chain. "That's so sad," she sighed. "Poor Linda. She deserved better than this."

"How did they seem when you interviewed them?" Zoe asked. Any lead was a lead, although she had by now become firmly sure that the selection of this Linda as a victim was nothing more than the random act of a stranger.

Shelley shrugged helplessly. "Surprised by the news. Not heartbroken. I don't think they were close."

Zoe fought back wondering who would care about her or come to see her body if she died, and replaced that thought instead with frustration. It was not difficult to find it. This was yet another dead end—literally. Linda had no more secrets left to tell them.

Standing around here commiserating with the dead was very nice, but it was not getting them any closer to the answers they were looking for.

Zoe closed her eyes momentarily and turned away, to the other side of the room and the door they had entered through. They needed to be on the move, but Shelley was still conversing with the coroner in low, respectful tones, discussing who the woman had been in life.

None of it mattered. Didn't Shelley see that? Linda's cause of death was very simple: she had been in an isolated gas station, by herself, when the killer came through. There was nothing else of note about her entire life.

Shelley seemed to pick up on Zoe's desire to go, drifting over to her side and politely distancing herself from the coroner. "What should we do next?" she asked.

Zoe wished she could say more in response to that question, but she couldn't. There was only one thing left to do at this point, and it was not the direct action that she wanted. "We will create a profile of the killer," she said. "Put out a broadcast over the neighboring states to warn local law enforcement to be on the watch. Then we will go over the files for the previous murders."

Shelley nodded, falling easily into step as Zoe headed for the door. It was not like they had far to go.

Up the stairs and out through the doors of the office, Zoe looked around and caught sight of the horizon line again, easily visible past the small collection of residences and facilities that made up the town. She sighed, folding her arms against her chest and whipping her head around to the precinct and where they were headed. The less time she spent looking at this place, the better.

"You don't like this little town, do you?" Shelley asked by her side.

Zoe felt a moment of surprise, but then again, Shelley had already proven herself to be both perceptive and attuned to others' emotions. Truth be told, Zoe was probably being obvious about it. She couldn't shake the foul mood that settled over her whenever she ended up somewhere like this. "I do not like small towns in general," she said.

"You just a city girl, or?" Shelley asked.

Zoe bit back a sigh. This was what happened when you had partners: they always wanted to try to get to know you. To dig up all of the tiny little pieces of the puzzle that was your past, and mash them together until they fit in a way that suited them. "They remind me of the place where I grew up."

"Ahhh." Shelley nodded, as if she saw and understood. She did not see. Zoe knew that for a fact.

There was a break in their conversation as they passed through the doors of the precinct, heading back toward a small meeting room that the locals had allowed them to use for their base of operations. Seeing that they were alone in there, Zoe placed a new pile of papers onto the table, starting to spread out the coroner's report along with photographs and a few other reports from officers who had been first on the scene.

"You didn't have a great childhood, then?" Shelley asked.

Ah. Maybe she did see, more than Zoe had given her credit for.

Perhaps she should not have been surprised. Why shouldn't Shelley be able to read emotions and thoughts the same way that Zoe could read angles, measurements, and patterns?

"It was not the best," Zoe said, tossing her hair out of her eyes and focusing on the papers. "And not the worst. I survived."

There was an echo in her head, a yell that came to her across time and distance. *Devil child. Freak of nature. Look what you've made us do now!* Zoe shut it out, ignoring the memory of a day locked in her bedroom as punishment for her sins, ignoring the long and hard loneliness of isolation as a child.

Shelley moved quickly opposite her, spreading out some of the photographs they already had, then lifting the files from the other cases.

"We don't have to talk about it," she said, softly. "I'm sorry. You don't know me yet."

That yet was ominous: it implied a time, even if it was in the distant future, when Zoe would be expected to trust her enough. When she would be able to spill all of the secrets locked inside of her since she was just a child. What Shelley did not know, could not guess from her gentle probing, was that Zoe was not going to tell anyone what had happened in her childhood—ever.

Except maybe that therapist that Dr. Applewhite had been trying to get her to see.

Zoe pushed it all away to give her partner a tight smile and nod, then took one of the files from her hands. "We should go over the previous cases. I will read this one, and you can read the other."

Shelley retreated to a chair on the opposite side of the table, looking at the images in the first file as they spread across the table, while chewing on one of her fingernails. Zoe tore her gaze away and focused on the pages in front of her.

"The first victim, killed in an empty parking lot outside a diner which had closed half an hour before," Zoe read aloud, summarizing the contents of the report. "She was a waitress there, a mother of two with no college education who had apparently stayed in the same area for her whole life. There was no sign of any forensic evidence of value at the scene; the methodology was the same, death by the wire and then the careful sweeping away of footprints and marks."

"Nothing to help us track him down, yet again," Shelley sighed.

"She had been locking up the place after cleaning up, on her way home after a long shift. The alarm was raised fairly swiftly when she did not arrive home as usual." Zoe flicked ahead to the next page, scanning the contents for value. "Her husband was the one to find her—driving out to look after she failed to answer her phone. There is a strong possibility that he contaminated evidence by grasping hold of his wife's body upon the discovery."

Zoe looked up, satisfied that this case was as empty of clues as the other. Shelley was still concentrating, playing with that pendant on her chain again. It was swallowed by her thumb and finger, small enough to disappear completely behind them.

"Is that a cross?" Zoe asked, when her new partner finally looked up. It was something to chat about, she thought. Fairly natural for an agent to speak to her partner about the jewelry she habitually wore, as it seemed she did. Right?

Shelley looked down at her chest, as if she had not realized what her hands were doing. "Oh, this? No. It was a gift from my grandmother." She moved her fingers away, holding it out so that Zoe could see the arrow-shaped gold pendant, complete with a tiny diamond set into the pointed head. "Lucky thing that my grandfather had good taste. It used to be hers."

"Oh," Zoe said, feeling a little relief wash over her. She had not realized how much tension she had been holding since she had first noticed Shelley pull out the chain and play with it. "An arrow for true love?"

"That's it." Shelley smiled. Then she furrowed her brow slightly, obviously having picked up on the shift in Zoe's mood. "Were you worried about me being overly religious or something?"

Zoe cleared her throat slightly. She had barely even recognized in herself that that was her reason behind asking. But of course it was. It had been a long time since she was that shy little girl with an overzealous God-fearing mother, but she still carried a fair amount of caution around people who considered the church to be the most important thing in their lives.

"I was just curious," Zoe said, but her voice was tight, and she knew it.

Shelley frowned, leaning over to pick up the next file from the table. "You know, we're going to have to spend a lot of time working together if we stay partners," she said. "Maybe it will go a little smoother if we don't keep things from each other. You don't have to tell me why you were worried about it, but I would appreciate the honesty."

Zoe swallowed, looking down at the file she had already finished reading. She gathered her pride, closing her eyes momentarily to shut off the voice telling her *no, not matching, one is approximately five millimeters thicker*, and met Shelley's gaze. "I do not have a good history with it," she said.

"Religion, or honesty?" Shelley asked with a playful smirk, opening her file. After a moment, during which time Zoe struggled with wondering what to answer, Shelley added: "That was a joke."

Zoe flashed her a weak smile.

Then she turned to the new case file and started examining the crime scene photographs, knowing this was the only thing that would take away the burning sensation traveling across her cheeks and neck and the awkwardness in the room.

"The second victim is another version of the same story," Shelley said, shaking her head. "A woman found murdered at the side of a road which wound along the edge of a small town. The kind of road you might walk alongside if you were heading home after a late night at work, which she was. She was a teacher...a bundle of marked papers spread around her where she had dropped them after her throat was cut by the wire garrote."

Shelley paused to scan through the photographs, finding the one with the papers. She held it up for a second, biting her lip and shaking her head. She passed it over to Zoe, who tried to feel the same level of pity and found that she could not. The papers made it no more poignant than any other death, in her mind. Indeed, she had seen far more brutal slayings that seemed more worthy of pity.

"She was found by a cyclist early the next morning. His eye caught the papers moving in the wind, trailing across the sidewalk and over to the body slumped half in long grass," Shelley summarized, recapping the notes in her file. "It looks as though she stepped to one side, as if helping someone. She was lured over there somehow. Damn...she was a good woman."

A number of scenarios flitted through Zoe's head: a fictitious lost dog, a stranger asking for directions, a bicycle with a loose chain, a request for the time.

"No footprints on the hard ground, no fibers or hairs on the body, no DNA under her fingernails. Just as clean as the other crime scenes," Shelley said, putting the file down in front of her with another sigh.

Whatever it had been that left her vulnerable—perhaps even just the element of surprise and a step off the sidewalk as she struggled against the wire around her throat—that was all they had to go on.

Zoe let her eyes rove over the paper aimlessly, trying to connect dots in ways that would fit all three cases.

Two happily married, one divorced. Two mothers, one who was childless. Different jobs for each of them. Different locations. One with a college degree, two without. No particular pattern to their names or connections through the companies they worked for.

"I don't see a link," Shelley said, breaking the silence between them.

Zoe sighed and closed the file. She had to admit it. "I do not either."

"So, we're back where we started. Random victims." Shelley blew out a breath. "Which means random next target, too."

"And a much lower chance that we can stop it," Zoe added. "Unless we can get enough of a working profile together to track this man down and catch him before he has a chance."

"So let's work on that," Shelley said, with a determination in the set of her face that actually gave Zoe a modicum of hope.

They set up a sheet of blank paper on an easel pad in the corner of the room and started going through what they knew.

"We can see his path," Zoe said; something she had already submitted out loud, and easy enough for anyone to work out. "He is on the move for some reason. What could that be?"

"Could be that he travels for work," Shelley suggested. "A trucker, a salesman or rep, something like that. Or he might be traveling just because he wants to. He could be homeless, too."

"Too many options for us to make a clear decision there." Zoe wrote *traveling* on the board, then tried to follow the implications. "He must sleep on the road. Motels, hotels, or perhaps in his car."

"If it's in his car, we don't have a lot of hope of tracking him down," Shelley pointed out, a downturn pushing the edges of her mouth. "He could be using fake names at the hotels, too."

"Not much to go on there. But he must travel in some way. By vehicle, judging on the distances between the kill sites and the time elapsed."

Shelley scrambled to tap on her cell phone, bringing up maps and checking the locations. "I don't think there's a clear train route. Maybe bus or car."

"That narrows it down somewhat," Zoe said, adding those possibilities to the list. "He could be a hitchhiker, though it is less common nowadays. What about his physical characteristics?"

"Traditionally, the garrote is used by those who are not physically muscular. So we could perhaps surmise that he is of a more average build."

Zoe was glad that Shelley had spotted it; one less thing for her to raise suspicions with. "Average, but not perhaps too small or petite. I feel that we have already become certain this is the work of a man. With too little strength, or height, the victims may have been able to overpower him and struggle free."

"And if he was too short, he wouldn't be able to reach well," Shelley added. "The victims were likely all killed while standing, which means he had to be able to easily reach their necks."

Zoe had to admit that she was impressed—even if only inside her own head. She wrote *average or above average height—five foot seven to six foot one*, based on the coroner's report, and *average or skinny build* on the board.

"Now, let us talk psychology," Zoe said. "There is something that is driving him to kill, even if it is not something that we would consider logical. If there is no real link between the victims, we have to look at that driving force as coming from within."

"They seem like crimes of opportunity to me. He only goes after women, perhaps because they are weaker. They are alone, defenseless, in an area not covered by working CCTV, and with a low possibility of being interrupted."

"I see two possibilities. The first is that he is driven to kill, and therefore seeks out these victims who fit the perfect profile for him to avoid being caught. For some reason, he is doing this now and all at once—so we would be looking at a trigger event," Zoe said, tapping the end of the pen against her chin. "The other possibility is that he is triggered specifically by these victims. In that event, he does not even know that he will kill them until it comes to the moment."

"In other words, he's either seeking out women to kill deliberately, or he is killing purely based on opportunity and something about the women themselves that sets him off," Shelley said, her eyes narrowed thoughtfully.

"Think about it." Zoe shook her head, pacing in front of the easel pad. "It is too perfect to be that random. One a night—that signifies a compulsion. If he was only driven to kill by trigger moments, we would see time between the attacks. He would be at home some nights, or just would not meet someone who set him off. No, this is deliberate and calculated. There is some reason why he has to kill each one, some message or ritual here."

She stepped forward again and wrote *one murder a day—ritual* on the board.

"What about the locations?" Shelley asked. "Maybe there's something there."

There was a map on the wall already, marked with three red pushpins where the three bodies had been found. Zoe regarded it for a moment, then used the edge of a piece of paper to line them up. It was a straight line between the first and the third. The second had deviated a little, but it was still on the overall path.

"What are those towns?" Shelley pointed toward the end of the piece of paper, after the last pin, at the settlements lying along the same path.

Zoe rattled off a list, reading them off the map, with a little deviation to either side in case he strayed off as he had before. "We should call the authorities in each of these towns. Make sure that they are all aware of what could be coming. Tightened security, and law enforcement with their eyes open, might help to catch him."

They both regarded their profile together in silence, thinking their own thoughts. On Zoe's part, she was trying to see the pattern. There were only three things that made sense to her: the fact that all were women, the timeline, or something to do with the locations. But what was it?

She thought back to the scattered, colorful candy that had been all over the ground at the gas station. Scattered not far from Linda's body, across the parking lot, across the path she must have taken to the rear of the building and back. It was so strange. It was altogether possible that some kid had dropped it earlier that day after stopping by with their parents, but…something about it was nagging at her.

Maybe it was simply the incongruity of it. Bright and cheerful candy at the scene of a brutal nighttime murder. Spots of color across a ground that was otherwise stained red. Maybe it didn't mean a thing at all.

"We do not have much," she sighed, at last. "But it is a start. Add to this that he is probably a young man, at least below middle age, according to statistics on the age at which serial killers begin their work, and we have narrowed it down enough to present something. I will ask the coroners to give us some more concrete numbers based on their findings, and we can at least give a description to be on the lookout for."

Which was not much of a consolation at all, she thought, if the killer was going to claim another victim tonight—and they were nowhere near close enough to do anything about it.

CHAPTER SIX

There would be another body tonight.

It was the fourth night, and that meant there must be a fourth body.

He had been driving for the whole day, moving closer and closer to his goal. Despite making good time, he was still growing more and more nervous as the sun moved overhead. When the evening set in, he had to be in the right place, or everything would go to waste.

He could not fail now.

He glanced over again at the cell balanced on his dashboard, hooked into a holder attached to his vents. The online map was slow to update out here, less signal to rely on. The highway was long and straight, at least, with no need to turn off. He would not get lost, nor would he miss his destination.

He knew precisely where he needed to go. It was all mapped out for him, written in the stars. Except for the fact that this pattern was far more precise than the mass of winking dots up there in the night sky, and far more easy to read. Of course, an expert could find those patterns, even way up there. But his pattern needed to be read even by those who did not normally see—and they would see, by the time he was finally done.

Who it would be was another question. Where, and when—yes, those were dictated by the pattern. But the who was more a matter of luck, and it was this that had him jiggling his leg up and down over the brake, his knee bouncing up and almost hitting the steering wheel each time.

He took a deep, calming breath, sucking in the rapidly cooling air. It was easy to sense that the sun was heading down across the sky, but it was not too late yet. The patterns had told him what he was supposed to do, and now he was going to do it. He had to trust in that.

The tires of his sedan thrummed endlessly across the smooth tarmac of the road, a steady background noise that was calming. He closed his eyes briefly, trusting the car to stay straight, and took another deep breath.

He tapped his fingers on the seal of the open window, falling into an easy repetitive beat, and breathed easier again. It would all be fine. Just as this car had stood him well for the years he had owned it, always reliable and dependable, the patterns would not let him down. So long as he checked the oil and took it in for servicing every now and then, it would run. And if he put himself into the right place at the right time, the patterns would be there.

They were all around him: the lines of the highway, stretching out into the distance straight and narrowing, telling him exactly where to go. The streaks of cirrus clouds which also seemed to point in the same direction, long fingers encouraging him onward. Even the flowers by the sides of the highway were bent, leaning forward in anticipation, like go-faster stripes swallowing the miles underneath his wheels.

It was all falling into place, just like the way the candy had fallen before he had killed the woman at the gas station. The way it had told him exactly what he needed to do next, and allowed him to see that he had already found the right place and the right victim.

The patterns would see him right, in the end.

Despite all of his mental reassurances, his heart was starting to race with anxiety as the sun began to fall lower and lower, dipping toward the horizon, and he still had not seen anyone suitable at all.

But now luck had found him again—the serendipity of being in the right place at the right time, and trusting the universe to do the rest.

She was walking backward along the shoulder of the highway, one arm stretched out to her side, thumb raised. She must have turned as soon as she heard him approach, his engine and the thrum of the wheels a giveaway long before they could see one another. She was carrying a heavy-looking backpack with a sleeping bag rolled up under it, and as he drew closer, he could see that she was young. No more than eighteen or nineteen, a free spirit on her way to a new adventure.

She was butter-soft and sweet, but that wasn't what mattered. Things like that never did. It was the patterns that mattered.

He slowed the car, coming to a stop just past her, then waiting patiently for her to catch up.

"Hi," he said, winding down the passenger's side window and inclining his head to look at her. "Are you looking for a ride?"

"Um, yeah," she said, looking at him mistrustfully, biting her lower lip. "Where are you headed?"

"Into the city," he said, gesturing ahead vaguely. It was a highway. There would be a city at the end of it, and she could fill in her own blanks as to which. "I'm glad I spotted you. Not many other cars on the road this time of day. It would be a cold night out here."

She gave a half-smile. "I would be fine."

He returned the smile broader, kinder, made it reach his eyes. "We can do better than fine," he said. "Hop in. I'll drop you outside a motel on the city limits."

She hesitated still; a young woman getting into a car with a man, alone—it didn't matter how nice he was. He understood that she would always be nervous. But she glanced up and down the road, and must have seen that even now, as the night was beginning to fall, there were no headlights in either direction.

She opened the passenger's side door with a gentle click, shrugging the backpack off her shoulders, and he smiled, this time for himself. All he had to do was trust, and things would work out the way the patterns told him they would.

CHAPTER SEVEN

"All right, listen up," Zoe said. She was already uncomfortable, and even more so when the idle chatter in the room ceased and every pair of eyes swung her way.

Having Shelley at her side did little to dissuade the feeling of awkward pressure, the weight of expectation hanging over her shoulders. The attention turned on her like a hose, palpable and shocking. The kind of thing she tried to avoid every day of her life, if she could help it.

But sometimes the job demanded it, and as much as she wanted to, she couldn't force Shelley to present a profile on her own. Not as the senior agent.

She took a breath, glancing across all of the officers seated in cramped rows of temporary chairs in the sheriff's largest briefing room. Then she looked away, finding a point on the far wall to speak to, something less threatening.

"This is the profile we are looking for," Zoe continued. "The male suspect will be around the height of five foot eleven, according to the calculations of all three coroners and what little physical evidence we found at the scenes. We also believe that he will be of thin to medium build. He is not particularly strong, forceful, or intimidating."

Shelley took over, stepping forward for her moment in the spotlight—something she seemed to relish rather than fear, her eyes taking on a gleam. "He will present as non-threatening to most people, until the moment of murder. We believe he has been able to entice his victims into conversations and even led them away from relative safety and into an open space where he could physically manipulate the situation to get behind them. He may even be charming, polite."

"He is not a local," Zoe added. "He will have out-of-state plates on his car. While we have not been able to determine his state of origin, he is on the move, and will likely continue to be."

Images of the women whose lives he had taken appeared on the projector screen behind them. They were all three alive, smiling at the camera, even laughing. They were normal, real women—not models or facsimiles of the same look or anything that would set them apart as special. Just women, who until three nights ago had all been living and breathing and laughing.

"He is targeting women," Zoe said. "One every night, in isolated places with little chance of being caught in the act or on surveillance footage. These are dark areas, away from the beaten track, places that give him the time and room to go through with the kill."

"How are we supposed to catch him with a profile like that?" one of the state cops piped up from the middle of the bristling copse of chairs in front of her. "There must be thousands of tall, thin guys with out-of-state plates around here."

"We realize this is not much to go on," Shelley stepped in, saving Zoe from the annoyance that had threatened to make her blurt out something unfriendly. "We can only work with what we have. The most useful course that we can take with this information at the present moment is to put out a warning to avoid isolated areas, and, particularly if approached by a man fitting this description, to be on guard."

"Across the whole state?" This question came from one of the locals, the small team working under the sheriff whose Missouri station they had taken over for both their investigation and this briefing.

Zoe shook her head. "Across several states. He has already moved through Kansas, Nebraska, and Missouri. That is a fair indication that he will continue to travel long distances in order to carry out his crimes."

There were small noises of disagreement throughout the room, mumblings and growls of discontent.

"I am aware that it is a large area," Zoe said, trying to be firm. "And I am aware that it is a vague warning. But we have to do what we can."

"Who's going to do the press conference?" the local sheriff asked. He had an air of battered authority about him, as if he were being crushed under the weight of all the other law enforcement officials crammed into his tiny station.

Zoe hesitated for a moment. She hated press conferences. She was criticized often for how stiff and emotionless she came across when talking about victims and the potential threat of more. She had done enough of them in her career to know that she never wanted to do another one again.

"My colleague, Special Agent Shelley Rose, will be talking to the media," she said, catching the way Shelley's head jerked up in surprise. "We will invite them to a televised conference later this afternoon."

As the various cops in the room began to clear away their chairs, the muttering in the room rising to full-level conversations, Shelley drew closer to Zoe with a nervous murmur. "I've never done a press conference before," she said.

"I know," Zoe replied. "I thought it would be a good chance for you to gain the experience. It is better now, while the case is fresh. The longer it goes on without being solved, the more vicious the reporters get. Trust me, I know. If we do not catch him before another press conference is required, I will take the lead then, as senior agent."

Shelley nodded, a thrill of excitement lighting up her cheeks with a faint blush. "Oh, god. Will you help me rehearse what to say? I've never even been on TV before, not even in the background."

Zoe couldn't help but smile. There was something about Shelley's excitement that was contagious, even if it would never come close to making her think that a press conference was an enjoyable thing. "Of course. I will help you put a script together."

❧ ❧ ❧

Later, Zoe stood behind a small podium, just in the camera shot, as Shelley addressed the assembled reporters. Given the scale of the case, there were news crews from across multiple states, and even national press organizations. Given the far-flung location and the short notice they had provided, there were fewer than there might have been. Perhaps just the right balance between enough publicity for the case and a small enough crowd that Shelley would not be overwhelmed.

"...So, we are asking you all to be vigilant," Shelley was saying. "Basic safety principles apply here, but it is more important now than ever to stick to them. Do not go into dark, isolated areas alone at night. Make sure that someone knows where you are at all times, and avoid going into a private area with strangers. Business owners, we ask you to repair and replace any CCTV systems which are not working. Be aware, be vigilant, and stay safe. We are working hard to catch the suspect behind these murders, but until he is found, we implore you to take all possible precautions."

Shelley paused, surveying the crowd of reporters, before continuing. "I will now take questions from members of the press."

A bespectacled man in an old-fashioned suit spoke up. "Kansas City Star," he announced. "Do you have a suspect in mind? Or have you been unable to identify the perpetrator?"

Shelley's confident demeanor faltered just a little. "We have not as yet identified a suspect. We are on his trail, however."

"Missouri State News," another reporter spoke up. "Where will he strike next?"

Shelley swallowed. "We can't at this moment be precisely sure of his location. This is why we are issuing the warning across several states. The suspect has been traveling long distances between crime scenes."

"You don't even know which state he's in?" the first reporter spoke again.

Shelley glanced uncertainly behind her, catching Zoe's eye. "At this time, we are steering clear of any assumptions," she said. "We believe we have some idea of his path, but it would be unwise to rule out a diversion or even a return to his previous sites."

There was a lot of muttering in the crowd, people swaying their heads closer to one another to confer, frowns plastered across almost all of the faces that Zoe could see. Leave them much longer, and they would be ready to eat Shelley alive. Zoe stepped forward quickly, approaching the microphone.

"No more questions at this time, thank you. We will announce another press conference in due course when we have more information," she said, taking Shelley by the elbow to gently steer her away.

Behind their retreating backs, the reporters exploded into a clamor, each of them shouting the questions they had not been given a chance to ask.

Zoe did not stop rushing forward, pulling Shelley with her, until they were back inside the doors of the station. They continued a short way along the corridor and ducked into their investigation room, where at last the hubbub was far enough away and behind enough doors that they could no longer hear it.

"Whew," Shelley exhaled, sitting down heavily. "That was tough."

"I wish I could tell you that it gets easier," Zoe said. "It does not. The press can be relentless. I imagine that we will find it difficult to move around without running into reporters from this point on."

Three killings was already a big news story. With this warning issued by the FBI, there was no doubt that more news crews would be flocking from miles around. They would trail Zoe and Shelley, trying to get to the next scene before anyone else, trying to find an exclusive angle.

It was perhaps the most exhausting, and Zoe's least favorite, aspect of the job.

But even with the threat of journalists hanging over their head, they had no time to pause or allow the investigation to rest.

"It's getting late. We should find a motel," Zoe said. "He will kill again tonight. Tomorrow, we should be rested and ready to move."

She could only hope that he would make a mistake tonight—the first one—that would allow them to draw nearer to catching him.

CHAPTER EIGHT

Rubie watched the small shrubs by the side of the highway flashing by the window. It was getting dark, the colors bleeding out of the world and reducing down to shades of gray. Fairly soon, she wouldn't be able to see much at all beyond the headlights of the car.

"What are you doing out here at this time of night anyway?" the driver asked. "You know it's not safe after dark."

"I know," Rubie sighed. "I didn't have much choice. I couldn't get away until Brent left to go meet his friends."

The driver glanced her way. His eyes flicked over the purple and green bruises on the left side of her face, then down to the yellowing marks still visible on her arm, before going back to the road. "Brent's the one who used you as a punching bag, I'm guessing."

Rubie flinched. To hear it said like that was so—so harsh. Like freezing cold water flung in her face. But it was true, after all.

"Sorry," the driver said, his voice softening. "I didn't mean that to be hurtful. The guy must be a complete douchebag if he's treating you like that."

Rubie looked out the window again, catching her own reflection. The swelling around her eye had gone down, but it still wasn't pretty. "No, you're right. He is. That's why I had to get away."

"What was his excuse?"

Rubie snorted, a laugh that couldn't quite make it past the pain. "Brent didn't need an excuse. He just got mad. I guess something happened at work. He always takes it out on me."

The driver shook his head, his fingers flexing on the steering wheel. "Asshole. He's lucky you were alone when I picked you up. If

54

he was trying to get somewhere, I would have left him in the dirt for doing that."

Rubie couldn't say that she was dismayed by the mental image. Brent deserved it. He deserved more than that. It made her feel just a touch safer. This driver seemed like the decent type—the type who didn't think that men should hit women.

"Sorry," he muttered after a moment. "I know I come on a bit strong. My mom was beaten by my stepdad. I grew up watching it. Best thing she ever did was grab me and get us away from him."

"I'm sorry," Rubie replied softly in return. No wonder he had been so eager to help her. He knew exactly what she was going through. "No kid should have to go through that."

"No woman either," he pointed out, glancing over at her.

Rubie found she was able to smile at him. It was such a little thing, but even to hear that from someone else meant the world. It meant she wasn't alone.

"So, you know where you're heading?" he asked.

"Yeah. I'm going to stay with family." Rubie clutched a little tighter at the duffel bag on her lap. It contained everything she had been able to carry: a few changes of clothes, some jewelry, and some mementos that she couldn't bear the thought of leaving behind. She guessed that these were her only possessions now. There was no chance that Brent would allow her to collect the rest of her things, not without trapping her and making her stay.

"They couldn't come and get you?"

"They don't know. I didn't have a way to get in touch with anyone. Brent wouldn't let me use my phone unsupervised."

Rubie put a finger to her face and probed her bruised skin gently, assessing the damage. She winced and drew in a sharp breath as she prodded a particularly painful spot. The pain was good. It reminded her why she had to get away. Why she couldn't give in and go back, for Brent to tell her how sorry he was and how it would never happen again.

It always happened again.

"Still, would have been safer to get a bus," the driver said. "I don't mean to go on about it, but hitchhiking isn't usually safe. Sure, it was me that picked you up this time. But it could have been anybody."

"I don't have enough money for a bus," Rubie said, resting her head against the cool glass. "Brent took it all. I just have a bit of change. Enough to get a couple of meals. That's all."

The driver hummed under his breath, a concerned noise. Rubie glanced at him sideways, wondering for a moment if he had been expecting payment for the ride. But that wasn't what was on his face. He looked genuinely upset for her. She was surprised, and her heart clenched in her chest for a moment at the thought that someone out there might actually care that she had been treated so badly.

"I'm sorry all this happened to you," he said. "You must have been terrified."

"I was," Rubie replied. "Thank you. For picking me up and being so kind."

He flashed her a quick smile. "Don't worry about it. Next time we see a diner, I'll stop off and get us some food. It'll be over an hour before we get to the next town. Might as well fuel up."

Rubie smiled back, resting against the window again and closing her eyes for a brief moment. Maybe this was it—the moment when her luck changed. Brent was miles behind her now, and he was never going to catch up. Not if she got to her sister. Lucy would keep her safe, and that would be the end of it. And here she was, with a guardian angel who would get her there, no matter what.

"Oh, damn," the driver said suddenly, hunching over the steering wheel with a frown. He turned on his indicators and drifted to the side of the road, where an exit led off the highway.

"What is it?" Rubie sat up straight, his voice putting her on alert.

"Something's wrong with the car," he said. He reached forward and tapped one of the dials on his dashboard, as if willing it to work. "I'm just going to pull over. Looks like an access road, so we should be fine at this time of night."

The wheels slowed to a halt, bumping up and down on the rough, uneven surface of the dirt road as the car stopped. It was fully dark out now, the moon hidden somewhere behind a cloud. All they could see in front of them were the beams of the headlights, illuminating a pathway that trailed into the distance.

The driver checked his GPS, tapping the screen a few times, zooming out and then back in on their position. "I don't know what's up with it, but I just lost power," he explained, leaning forward over the dash again to examine the symbols lighting up. "Sorry about this. It's a pretty old car."

"That's fine," Rubie said. After all, she could hardly complain. But this wasn't ideal. She didn't want to be stuck in the middle of nowhere because the one car that agreed to pick her up had broken down. She didn't have much chance of getting another ride in the dark.

The driver turned the ignition off and then on again, tilting his head to listen closely to the sound of the engine. "How much do you know about cars?" he asked.

Rubie gave a short laugh. "I don't even have my driver's license," she said.

The driver gave her a wry grin, a look that seemed to acknowledge how awkward their situation was but also that there was nothing to be done about it. "I can't hear the engine properly from inside here. Could you do me a favor? If you pop the hood, you should be able to listen out for a rattle. That might tell me what's going on."

Rubie eyed the darkness warily. It looked cold out there, not to mention that they were in the middle of nowhere. She wasn't an idiot. She had seen movies.

But then again, movies weren't reality. There wasn't a whole lot of choice. If she didn't help him out with getting the car going again, they would be stuck here for even longer. And this guy had helped her out, picked her up off the side of the road and listened to her story. He was sympathetic, pleasant to talk to.

Rubie squared her shoulders and reached for the door handle. "Just a rattle, right?"

"That's it. I'll rev the engine when you've got the hood up. Then just shout if you hear something."

Rubie nodded, getting out into the chill air. The whole area around them was quiet, only the small, subtle sounds of bugs going about their nightly business. There was no sound of another engine, except maybe so far away that it was hard to tell whether she was really hearing anything. The road was practically empty. Definitely no chance of getting another ride.

The driver had already popped the hood, and Rubie lifted it, a little gingerly, trying not to get grease on her hands. It wasn't as though she had enough clothes that she could afford to ruin the ones she was wearing.

She realized, even as she did it, that from this angle she could no longer see the driver. In the silence she heard the noise of his door opening and pulled back a little, concerned.

Maybe this had all been a trap. Maybe he looked at her and knew she was someone he could abuse, push around, take what he wanted from. He was going to get out of the car now and beat her, leave her lying on the ground with her shorts around her ankles when he was done.

"Shout if you hear it," he repeated, his voice coming from inside the car. The engine revved, making her jump and catch a scream in her throat.

God, she was paranoid. Brent had left her jumping at shadows, suspicious of everyone and everything. It was going to take her a long time to get over this, to stop suspecting strangers of harboring ill intent. The driver was a good man. He'd shown that by picking her up, and by his anger at how Brent had treated her. She had to keep that in mind, and help him out with the engine so that she could get to Lucy sooner rather than later.

Where else was she going to go, anyway? There was nowhere to run. He was the only car who bothered to stop for her, and there hadn't been anyone else on the road for a long time. Like it or not—and she admitted to herself that maybe she didn't like it, a shiver running down her spine—she was stuck with him.

Better make the most of it.

She peered down into the dim engine, trying to make something out. It was all darkly glistening metal, most of it greased up and black, not even reflecting a dull glint from the headlight beams still blasting out into the darkness. Rubie was almost blind from the light, the contrast so strong that it blotted everything else out.

The engine stopped revving, the noise fading out into silence. As it did and the quiet of the night returned, her ears buzzed. The loud noise right next to her had blotted everything else out, and just how the headlights left her blind, she could barely hear a thing with the contrast.

"I didn't hear any rattle," she called out, hoping it would help. If there was nothing wrong with the engine, maybe they would be able to get going again. It wasn't a new car—maybe it just needed a moment to rest and it would be good to go again.

Rubie shivered, rubbing her hands over her arms. The driver hadn't said a thing, and he wasn't revving the engine again either. She peered down into the darkness of the engine once more as if it could tell her something, and flinched when the reflected light on the engine was blocked by a deep shadow falling over her.

She heard his step behind her, a loose stone moving away from his foot, and jumped upright. "I didn't…" she began, meaning to say that she'd had no idea he was behind her, but her heart was racing with the shock of his presence and she lost the words.

He was looking at her, just looking at her. His expression was almost blank, frighteningly so.

"Wh-what's that in your hand?" she asked, gesturing down to the wire that was illuminated fully in the headlights. "Will it…fix the…?"

She trailed off, beyond shaken now. In a flash, she remembered something she had seen when he had picked her up off the side of the road. Something she had dismissed at the time when he spoke, friendly enough, and offered her a wide smile.

Something like hunger, or a cruel kind of joy, like a wolf looking down at a trapped rabbit.

Rubie turned on her heel, wanting to get back into the car now, wanting to get back where it was warm and safe. Where he had been a perfect gentleman and empathized with her story and shared his own past, something that made them equal and the same. If she could just get back inside—

Rubie reached up instinctively as something connected with her neck—something light and thin but sharp, hurting her fingers as she grabbed at it. What was that? The wire? She pulled and tugged at it, feeling the source somewhere behind her, the heat coming from a body that was not her own.

She hit out blindly, directing her elbows and feet backward, struggling to find him and catch him off-guard. He was hissing under his breath, cursing, telling her to stay still. She wouldn't stay still. No. She forced her elbow back again, a desperate aim into the darkness, and felt it connect heavily with something.

The driver grunted in pain, and the force around her neck relaxed for just a second. Rubie dropped down to her knees, then scrambled forward, finding her way clear. Whatever he had wrapped around her was gone. She kicked off from the ground and sprang forward, at a right angle to the beams of the headlights, avoiding the easily illuminated path they provided.

Something was hot and heavy on her chest as she ran, gasping for breath already in the cold air that stung like ice in her lungs. What was that? Her hand flew up, feeling wetness all across her shirt, following it up as her feet stumbled on the uneven ground. She could not hear him coming after her, but she ran as fast as she could, as fast as she dared to trust her feet to manage. The wetness—it was coming from her neck—coming from where she had felt the pressure earlier—a wound that began to pulse with pain as soon as her fingers found it.

There was blood—so much blood—right across her chest, dripping down over her stomach. She felt the hot rivulets running down to splash onto her legs as they pumped desperately for distance, putting as far between herself and the driver as she could.

The blood wouldn't stop, so much of it. Rubie grasped at her neck with both hands as she ran, sacrificing the added balance and mobility of her arms, trying to hold it all in. There was a line that stretched from one side to the other, wrapping around, oozing and leaking more and more with each passing moment.

Without her eyes or her balance, Rubie stumbled, one foot catching on something that felt like a rock or a hard tuft of ground. She fell heavily, unable to break her fall, the wind rushing out of her as her elbows hit the ground first. At the same time she felt a gush, a feeling like water from a tap bursting out beneath her fingers.

She wasn't going to give up. No. She had to get away—keep going—as far away from him as she could. She didn't dare look around to see if he was still standing in the light from the car, or if he was only steps behind her, ready to grab her again. She couldn't waste time. Rubie got her feet underneath her and pushed up again, only to fall, sagging, her legs refusing to work.

Everything felt strange—loose—like she was made of jelly all of a sudden, her arms and legs flopping like dead fish when she tried to move them. The one thing she knew she could feel was the heat of the blood seeping out of her neck, staining the ground now, pouring in such quantities that she could not comprehend it.

Rubie lifted her head to look into the distance, the lights of the town where her sister lived still just a speck on the horizon. So far away that it might as well have been the stars. The wound on her neck opened like a mouth to pour out another gush of blood, and she felt her face hit the ground, no longer strong enough to hold it up.

She only registered dimly that she could no longer feel the cold before there was nothing left to feel at all.

CHAPTER NINE

Zoe was dismayed to find that the motel was even shabbier on the inside than it had looked from the outside.

"Only the finest for the FBI," Shelley joked. "That's why they call us 'special' agents, right?"

Zoe grunted, turning back from her examination of the threadbare sofa in the lobby just in time to see the receptionist returning. "Here's your key," he said, tossing one plastic card onto the surface of the counter. It slid over toward them, stopping just before it teetered off the edge.

"Thanks," Shelley said, picking it up and lifting her hand in a gesture of acknowledgment.

Zoe didn't think his customer service skills warranted even that.

The man said nothing. He slumped back into his chair and grabbed up his cell from in front of him, resuming whatever activity he had been engaged in when they entered.

"You know where we can get a decent bite to eat at this time of night?" Shelley asked.

"Diner 'bout five miles down," he said, lifting his chin in the approximate direction without looking up.

Shelley thanked him again, to as little response as the first time. They left him where he was, Zoe leading her away before she could try to start another conversation with the world's surliest clerk, heading back out into the cold night of the parking lot.

"Should we go for dinner?" Shelley asked. "Or set up the room first?"

"We should put our bags in, at least," Zoe said, sighing. She rubbed the back of her neck, stiff and sore from the long day and the driving they had done. "Then food."

"So much for getting on a plane before the day was out," Shelley remarked, hefting the key and examining it for the room number. She led them across the lot to a door much like all of the others in the long, low building, unlocking it with a swipe.

"It looks like this was more of a complex case than expected," Zoe agreed. The mild words hid the anger she was harboring toward herself. She should have been able to solve this one, read the numbers and taken him down. Not leave him the chance to kill again. If someone died tonight, it would be on her.

The room was small, two single beds placed less than a foot apart with old-fashioned floral bedspreads. The kind that had probably been purchased in the eighties, or even earlier, and washed over and over again until they were thin and scratchy. At least, Zoe hoped they had been washed.

She kicked one leg of the bedframe, eyeing it warily to see how much it shifted. It felt good, but not good enough. Zoe could probably have kicked the whole place until her leg hurt, and it still wouldn't work out the frustration she felt. She should have been home by now, not sitting in a motel and waiting for a killer to claim another victim that she could do nothing to prevent.

She thought of Euler and Pythagoras, and hoped they were all right. She had a delayed-release feeder set up for nights like these, but the cats were too clever for their own good. Once before, they had broken into it and eaten half a week's supply in one night. She'd come home a few hours later to find them lying bloated and happy, so full they could only wave their tails in response to her voice.

"Ready?" Shelley asked, her voice quiet. Perhaps feeling that Zoe was not in the mood for this, for any of this.

Zoe nodded and allowed her partner to lead the way. It was with no great joy that she approached the diner, seeing the lights an oasis in the darkness of the rural area, already mostly shut down for the night. Only a few cars were parked outside in the small lot, and the large windows on all sides of the building allowed them to see just a few patrons sitting to eat or drink coffee. It made her catch her breath in her throat, memories flooding in unbidden of diner meals from her childhood.

Zoe stifled a groan of complaint as they walked inside. It was your typical small-town diner. Wipe-clean tables and green-covered seats and booths, an attempt at kitsch 1950s stylings that contrasted against the modern appliances and images of local sports teams on a bulletin board. The two tired-looking waitresses, both middle-aged women, wore nondescript uniforms that were neither stylish nor well-fitting. Her eyes told her that one was wearing one size exactly too small, the other one size too large. She blinked, shooing the numbers away. She just wanted to eat and go to bed.

Zoe slid into a booth and examined the menu. At times it could be soothing to see a familiar list of items and know what you wanted to order, but here it was grating. It was a standard, generic offering of diner fare, the kind of all-day pancakes and burgers you could get at any similar spot in the country. It could easily have been the precise menu offered by the diner in Zoe's own hometown, where she had slunk sullenly after church, following her parents for their weekly celebratory meal.

Not that it had ever been a real celebration, for her.

She stared at the menu without reading it, feeling her mother's hot gaze on the top of her head, the glare she would always look up to find. Silently, as she always did when faced with a menu, she let the numbers fill her head—telling her the predicted cost per weight of each meal, the number of calories to expect, which held more fat and which more sugar. A pointless exercise, because Zoe never used any of that to choose her meals. She had learned long ago just to pick something she liked and put the numbers away.

"Can I get you some coffee?" their waitress asked, pausing at their table with a jug in hand. Zoe held out her cup wordlessly to have it filled, while Shelley assented and gave her thanks. With a promise to come back for their food order soon, the waitress was gone again, heavy footsteps slapping the linoleum in flat shoes.

"What are you getting?" Shelley asked. "I can never choose. I'm so bad at picking what I want to eat. It all sounds good."

Zoe shrugged. "Burger, probably."

"With a side of fries?"

"Comes with it."

Shelley scanned the menu again a few more times before nodding and closing it. "Sounds good enough."

Zoe lifted her gaze to momentarily analyze the alcoholic, the long-distance trucker, and the family man with no desire to go home before deciding the other patrons of the diner were not worth looking at. She turned her eyes to the salt shaker, measuring the precise amount of salt left within it and comparing it with the sugar, before tuning out even that.

The numbers weren't helping. The case was still unsolved, nothing left behind by the criminal that she could use even with her unique abilities. Now she was stuck in this two-horse town for at least another day, looking at things that reminded her of her childhood and all the things that her mother had been at pains to point out were wrong with her. All the while, somewhere, some woman might be fighting for her life, losing it in an empty parking lot or by the side of the road.

"If you don't like it here, we'll go somewhere else tomorrow," Shelley said, offering Zoe an attempt at a bright smile. "Somewhere not so small-town. Maybe we can order takeout to the motel."

Zoe glanced up. Once again, Shelley had surprised her with just how insightful she could be.

"This place is just fine. I apologize if I am being unpleasant. I was hoping we would solve this one quickly and go home. I do not want any more people to die."

"Me, too." Shelley shrugged. "We'll get there. It's all right, though. You don't have to put on a customer service face with me. I can tell you're not comfortable here."

"I did not wish to distract us from the case by bringing up my own problems," Zoe said, twisting her mouth. "I suppose I was not doing a great job of hiding it."

Shelley laughed. "I've only been working with you for a little while, Z, but I'm starting to see the signs. There's a difference between you being quiet because you're, well, you, and then you being quiet because you're not comfortable."

Zoe looked down at her coffee, pouring exactly one teaspoon of sugar from the shaker without measurement and stirring it, careful not to clink her spoon against the side of the cup. "It's too much like home here."

"I'm not trying to push you. I meant what I said—you don't need to tell me about it," Shelley said, taking a sip of hers black. "But you can. If you want."

Zoe shrugged. How much to tell? She had not changed her mind about reserving the details, except perhaps for the therapist. But her issues were affecting her work, and Shelley deserved to know why. At least a little bit of why. "My mother was manipulative," she said, simply. Best to leave out the part where she accused her of being the devil's spawn. "My father was a bystander, at best. I was legally emancipated as a teenager."

Shelley let out a low whistle. "It must have been bad, if you had to go that far to get away from them."

Zoe shrugged again. She sipped at her coffee, feeling the slight discomfort from the heat, setting it carefully back down on the table. She was never good at talking about herself. The few times she had tried as a child, her mother had made it clear that the things she felt and saw were not normal.

"I hope I'm never like that," Shelley sighed. "Or even close to it. I want to be a good mother. Of course, I'm not going to be at home as often as I could be. But I still want to do well."

Zoe took in Shelley's face, pensive and distracted. "You have children?"

"One." Shelley smiled, her face coming to life with warmth. "My daughter."

"What is her name?"

"Amelia. It was hard, going into training and then coming to work. I decided to change careers after I went on maternity leave.

As much as I think I've found my calling, it was tough to leave her at home."

"Your partner is looking after her?" Zoe asked.

"My mother. During the day, at least. My husband works in an office job, nine to five. He's always there for her on the weekends." Shelley sighed. "We need both the money from working."

Zoe considered her for a long moment. She ducked her eyes back down to her cup. "I do not think you could be a bad parent," she said at last. "You will never be anything like my mother."

"Thank you." Shelley smiled. The relief in her expression was palpable. "I needed to hear that."

Zoe thought about Shelley's little girl, and the fact that each of the victims had a mother once, and fought the urge to go back out into the night to continue the search for their killer. She would be no help to anyone if she didn't get enough sleep to think clearly, enough nutrition to keep her body going. That was what was important tonight, while they had no real leads to speak of.

Somehow, knowing that Shelley was a mother, and that she cared greatly about her little family—enough to worry about it so much—made her rise higher in Zoe's estimation. The empathy that she had for victims and their families was not an act. Shelley had genuine compassion in her. It was something Zoe wished she had more of. Perhaps Shelley was exactly the kind of partner she needed.

Especially if, tomorrow morning, she was going to have to face the family of another victim, and explain to them why she had not caught the killer.

CHAPTER TEN

Rubie faded back into consciousness, the world coming into focus again. Soil underneath her face. Grass, short and sharp blades, uncomfortable under her cheek. She moved her eyes, seeing the lights of the town in the distance, and then around her, the trees, rising dark and tall, blocking her view to the left and right.

She must have stumbled into the woods. She barely remembered. All she had been able to focus on was the blood, falling hot and wet in pools down her body.

How long had she been out? It was still dark, still cold, and she was still alive. She pressed her hand to her neck with the smallest of movements and found it still liquid. Not long, then. If she had been bleeding for a long time, she would be dead.

Rubie's ears pricked at a sound nearby, and she instinctively slowed her breathing, making a conscious effort not to exhale loudly. The slower she breathed, the less the blood pulsed out of her neck. It was so deep, the air rushed through. She pressed her hand harder against the red-hot line of pain, trying to keep it all in.

Footsteps. It was his footsteps. Slow, cautious, one foot after another. Not blundering through the woods but moving carefully. Searching. Searching for her.

A wild spike of fear dizzied through her and she fought to keep her breathing under control, to stay as quiet as possible. He was getting closer, moving right toward her. Oh god, if he found her again. Oh god, it would be over.

Rubie held on tight to her neck, feeling stars in her vision every time her grip slipped and the wound eased open again, letting out another flood. Every part of her body wanted to give in to the waiting darkness, to go once again into the sweet unknowing of unconsciousness. But she knew. Rubie knew that if she went down again, she would never come back up.

The footsteps were so close that she stopped breathing at all. She held herself still, as still as she could, until the only movement in her whole body was the blood driven heartbeat by heartbeat out of her neck. She waited. How long could she hold her breath before she had to make another sound? What if he could see her? How long until he killed her?

The footsteps kept moving, and when Rubie realized they were heading past her, into another direction, deeper into the woods, she gasped out a breath at last. Her body came back to life, all the aches and pains flooding her, reminding her of the cold earth and the cold air and the warmth seeping out of her pulse by pulse.

If she could stop the bleeding, she had a chance. She could stumble out of here, even crawl if she had to. It was a long time until daybreak, a long time before he would have the benefit of the sun to spot her with. She could be in town by then, at the hospital, safe and secure. She could make it out. She was strong enough.

If she could just stop the bleeding.

Rubie tried to think, forcing her dull and frozen brain into action. A bandage—that was what she needed. Her hands were slippery with blood, and weak from the loss of it. She couldn't grip the wound closed, not well enough. A bandage would hold her together.

But where would she get a bandage?

Not a medical bandage—it could be anything. A strip of fabric. Duct tape. She'd seen that in a film. Staples, even. No, not staples or tape—think. Think. Think of something that she actually had access to.

Clothes! Her clothes! They were made from—made from fabric. What was she wearing? Jean shorts—that was why her legs were so cold. A tee, tight to her body and small. The only thing between her stomach and the cold ground. A zip-up hoodie, open, the hood pooled against the back of her neck, keeping her warm there.

Her bag! She had a scarf in her bag—but it was—no—back in the car...

Okay, think. The clothes she was wearing, these were all she had. The tee—the fabric was thin. Maybe easier to rip. She could tear it, take a whole section off the bottom. That was what they did in movies, right? Just tear it right off with their hands.

Rubie gathered her remaining strength, taking one hand away from her neck, and pushed against the cold earth. Damp soil pushed up between her fingers, oozing into the spaces, before she finally began to move. Slowly, and then in a rush all at once when gravity came to her aid, she flopped over onto her back. The impact rocked her back and forward, shaking the air out of her system.

There. One step closer. Now the blood was running back, trickling down across her neck and back toward her hair, and she felt she could let go for a moment to fumble for the fabric of her shirt.

She pulled and strained, but her normal strength was gone from her. Her movements were ineffective, her hands slipping and the fabric gliding out from between her frozen fingertips.

Think, Rubie, think.

The seams—they were the weak points.

She fumbled around for the side seam, finally finding it and taking hold of each side in her hands. She grasped and pulled, taking a deep breath and using everything she had—and the seam ripped, the stitches popping and unraveling with a sound like Velcro.

Rubie wanted to cry. She'd done it. But it was only the first step.

Step.

She heard it—his footsteps.

They were getting louder.

He was coming back.

He hunted for her relentlessly, with an energy born of twin flames of fear and anger. This was not the plan. She was *ruining* the plan.

This stupid girl should have died where he took her, where she was supposed to. Why did she have to run away like that? And into the woods, no less?

It was dark, but he did not want to risk turning on the flashlight on his cell. If he did, he might be spotted from the road. Someone could identify his car, then, and the police would crash down on him, APBs and roadblocks and records searches. He had switched off the car lights and the engine, left it sitting in darkness, where he hoped no one would pass by.

But even more of a risk than a driver or passenger happening to look over and spot his car was the girl. She would ruin the pattern if she escaped, but it was more than that. She knew his face. She would be able to describe his car. Maybe she had even gotten a look at the plates before she accepted his ride.

If she got out of the woods and got to the authorities, they would find him in no time at all.

He stalked through the trees with an ever-increasing sense of desperation, a growl rising in his throat as he moved further and further from the road. He couldn't see anything. The splashes of blood on the ground near the car had been encouraging, but out here the light of the moon did not penetrate the branches, and he could no longer follow the trail.

He knew he had cut her—but how much? If it was only a shallow wound, she could make it all the way to town. Maybe before he found her. If he ever found her. Maybe she was halfway there, even now.

He stopped moving, standing still, listening to the swaying and rustling of the trees in a light wind that passed through. This was hopeless. If there wasn't some kind of miracle, he wasn't going to find her in time. It was all going to be over.

There—what was that sound? He whirled around, his heartbeat picking up pace, pounding so loudly in his ears he was afraid it would drown out any further clues.

He moved in the direction that it had come from, faster now, forgetting care in exchange for haste. What had it been? A ripping noise, he thought, like fabric coming apart. Not an animal noise. Not a bird or a squirrel or anything else—a girl.

He moved forward blindly in the darkness, seeing only the very nearest objects, holding his hands out in front of him so that he would not hit a tree while he concentrated on the ground at his feet. There—was that a blood splatter?

He took a glance behind him at the road and hesitated, assessing the risk. He switched on the screen of his cell, using that dim light only, and squatted down. Yes—blood! He moved the light, following it forward, tilting it up and up and up until—

The light hit her body, shining from her eyes, glistening in the wet pools around her and the trickle still oozing from her neck.

He smiled at last and rushed forward, squatting over her, careful to avoid stepping in the blood.

She was breathing still. But it was shallow and low, her eyes already taking on a glassy look. Her hands, which were down by the hem of her ripped T-shirt, were bloody and shaking, a minute tremble that twitched through them. She was staring up at him; with comprehension or not, he could not tell.

There was blood all around her. All over her. She was soaked in it. He had managed to cut deeply, before she hit him and escaped. It was still coming out of the deep slice along her neck.

Her hands stilled. He leaned forward, over her, closer and closer, until his face was only inches from her own. He concentrated, stilling his own body, staying as quiet as he could.

She was no longer breathing.

She had bled out, at last.

For one second he wanted to crow with victory, and in the next he wanted to erupt with rage. This was wrong—all wrong. She had died in the wrong place! The bitch had ruined everything, everything! The pattern was broken, wrong, destroyed!

He stood and kicked out at the body, hitting her in the side with a satisfying thunk, the noise reminding him of the sound meat made when hit with a tenderizing hammer.

Not quite satisfying enough, given that she had broken his pattern, and destroyed everything that he had been working for.

He stepped back, breathing hard, and let his eyes fall over the scene as he used the light from his cell to examine her. The blood would need some attention. There was too much evidence at the present moment, too many signs to direct the investigators where to go.

But—what was this...? Now that he looked closer...yes, she must have rolled away, pushing herself from where she had originally fallen. And there, blooming out in almost perfect symmetry, the blood had spilled from her neck. It was...beautiful. No, now that he looked even closer, it *was* symmetrical, a perfect blossom, like a Rorschach blot.

A pattern.

His breathing began to slow, to even out again, along with the pace of his racing heart. Here was a pattern, even now. A pattern to show him that everything was okay.

The girl had not ruined everything. No, this was only a small deviation from the plan. He still committed the murder exactly where he had planned to. She had run on ahead, but she was already dead from the moment his wire slipped around her neck—like a chicken, the body still moving after the head was gone.

The pattern was still intact.

It was just like the old man, the one they hadn't found yet, up at the farmhouse where no one had seen him for days. He had tried to run, too. In the end, it had not changed a thing. The pattern began there, and here, it was able to continue. Like divine providence, keeping him on track, allowing him to realize his work fully.

His moment of celebration was short-lived. Now that he knew everything was going to be fine, there were steps he had to take. The pattern would continue, and that meant he could not leave behind any evidence for them to find and stop him before he finished tomorrow's kill—or the day after, or the day after that.

The first thing was the blood trail. If he could take care of that, he could drive away before the sun came up, and no one would be any the wiser.

He stood straight, cracking his shoulders back, rolling them toward his spine. There was physical labor to be done again, which he did not mind at all. It purified the scene, made the pattern the only thing that was left. Removing all traces of himself was like an artist stepping back and allowing a painting to speak for itself. It was an act removed of ego, a reiteration of his devotion to the pattern, his belief that it was bigger than himself.

He found a dead branch nearby, the twigs and leaves still barely hanging on, a recent break. Perfect for sweeping away the marks from a crime scene. He hefted it and began to sweep away some of his own footsteps around the body, careful to walk backward, following her trail.

He stiffened as the gentle swish-swish of the branch was interrupted by another sound. He froze, stilling his whole body to listen again, pressing a button to deaden the light from his cell. What was that? A bird call?

No—there it was again: a human voice, and no mistaking it.

He listened intently, turning his head to catch the right direction of the wind, tuning his senses as much as he could. He peered ahead, as if seeing the source of the sound might make it clearer. There were voices, all right. Two men. Moving closer, maybe. Slowly, but surely.

"This is it, here." One of the men.

Something from the other, too quiet to hear.

"Oh, rest your grumbling. Any critter worth its pelt knows we're here already. They hear our steps. Bit of talking won't make a difference. When we're in the stand, I'll be quiet."

He squinted, analyzing the words. Hunters, most likely. Setting themselves up in tree stands to wait for the woods to adjust to their presence, for small and defenseless things to forget they were there. A long waiting game.

He couldn't outwait them.

He had to get out, and do it now.

His tracks were still intact, the blood trail leading right from his car to the body. But there was no doing anything about it. He had to go, before they heard a cracked twig or a swish of the makeshift broom and saw him. Or even worse, shot at him, thinking him to be some kind of beast. It was time to leave, and there was nothing else he could do.

He fled back to his car in quick, careful steps, minding where he stood, never close enough to the blood trail to risk stepping in it and leaving imprints behind. He strayed to the side to discard the branch away from the path she had left, hoping it would avoid notice. One fallen branch among all the other fallen branches. None of this was finished—but it would have to be, or else he would have to stop now, before he was done with the rest.

His work was far from done. There were three more who had to die—and he wasn't going to stop until they were all bled out on the ground, and the pattern was complete.

CHAPTER ELEVEN

Zoe emptied her first coffee of the day and threw the Styrofoam cup into the trash can. It bounced against the back edge with a satisfying finality, dropping out of sight to rest alongside many of its brothers and sisters.

"The coffee here is dreadful," Shelley remarked, staring miserably into her own cup.

Zoe could not help but agree.

She rubbed at her eyes, willing them to open wider. Early morning starts were always rough after late night finishes, but she had grown used to them over the years. The routine was simple: pump your body full of enough caffeine to get you moving, and your brain will follow.

Still, watching the security camera footage they had pulled from everywhere within a five-mile radius of the gas station—which amounted to very few files, given its location—was a challenge of even her early bird mentality. Her eyes either picked up all kinds of numbers that were irrelevant and distracting, or wanted to droop shut at the sheer boredom of seeing nothing for minutes on end.

She darted her vision between the timestamp at the bottom of the screen and the main view incessantly, watching time creep on closer to the murder. No vehicles had yet entered or left the field of view of the truck stop. It was a more populated place than the gas station, even at night, but the trucks in the parking lot had mostly settled in for a sleep. Nothing moved.

A blue car flashed by, on the small portion of road that was visible to the side of the parking lot. It moved fast, and even with her finger on the pause button, Zoe only managed to hit it once it was gone.

She tracked back, frame by frame, until it was contained within the small section of the screen that held the road. She checked the timestamp. It was perfectly within the window. The driver would have had time to get to the gas station, commit the murder, and be gone in line with the timeframe they had narrowed it down to.

She played it forward again, watching the time flash by. Minutes turned into hours. Nothing else traveled the lane that she could see on the camera.

She went back, returned to the precise moment when the car could be fully seen. Zoe squinted, peering so closely that her nose almost bumped the screen, trying to take down the license plate. Was that an O or a D? She flicked back and forth between the frames, trying to make it out.

"I have got something," she said, pulling Shelley's attention. "There was a car caught on the security camera on the approach to the gas station. It works for the timing, and no other vehicles appear to pass by for at least an hour. I have the plate. I just need to run it through the database."

Shelley's face brightened with excitement, as she hurried around to look over Zoe's shoulder at the frozen image. "That could be him, Z," she breathed.

"I will bring up the details," Zoe said, stopping the video playback file and opening up a program that would allow her to run the plates through the national database. Her first try, with the D, gave them nothing. The O turned up a hit.

"Jimmy Sikes," Shelley read out loud. She returned to her own computer, where the FBI software was already waiting for input of names. "Got him. Let's see ... oh, wow, Z, he has a record. He just got released on probation a few months ago."

"What for?" Zoe asked.

"Assault," Shelley read, turning wide eyes to her. "Violent past. You think this could be the guy?"

Zoe raised her eyebrows, thinking about it. "Could be. He was in the area, and having a criminal record certainly makes it more likely. We need to talk to him immediately."

"His probation address is listed as his sister's residence. Should I call her?"

Zoe nodded her assent, watching how Shelley fumbled breathlessly for the desk phone and input the numbers before taking a calming breath. She was excited. She was still green, still exhilarated by the prospect of a solve. Zoe enjoyed closing a case as much as the next person, but she had also been in the game long enough to know that identifying a suspect was nowhere close at all to putting it to bed.

"Hello, am I speaking to Manda Sikes?" Shelley said into the receiver, her eyes darting away from Shelley and down to a blank page of her notebook in concentration. "Hello, Manda. My name is Special Agent Shelley Rose with the FBI. I'm calling in regards to your brother, Jimmy."

There was a pause as Manda spoke. Shelley nodded, even though the other woman could not see her, opening and closing her mouth several times as she waited for a moment to cut in.

"No, I understand. This is not in regards to his assault conviction. We're actually looking to speak with him about another case."

Another pause. Longer, this time. Shelley glanced up at Zoe in alarm at whatever Manda was saying.

"So you haven't seen him since then? And that was—right, five days ago. He hasn't made contact of any kind? You've tried calling him? Okay. Right. Could you tell me his cell number?"

Shelley made notes on the pad, scratching out a number in quick strokes of her pen. She exchanged a few more words with Manda before hanging up, then gave Zoe a raised eyebrow.

"Jimmy Sikes has not returned home for a number of days?" Zoe asked.

"Not since before our first murder. Manda says that she's tried calling him over and over again, but his cell is switched off. She thought we were his probation worker trying to track him down at first."

"So, it is looking more and more likely that Jimmy may be involved with our case. I will liaise with the team back at HQ to get a trace on his cell, and search for flags for his license plate."

Shelley nodded, putting her pen down. "I'll finish going through the security footage we have. It might not show us anything else, but at least we'll know for sure that that part is ticked off."

Zoe moved quickly, placing the necessary calls and entering data into her computer, logged into the FBI's databases. This was a high-priority case, and with a judge already on standby to sign off on search warrants, things were going to go fast for them. Still, it took a number of hours, impatient tapping of pens and jiggling of knees, before they had the information they needed.

"Here we go," Zoe said, printing off the map and dragging it out of the machine almost before it had finished. "These are our points of interest. Every location where we have been able to track Jimmy Sikes over the last few days."

Shelley crowded next to her, shoulder to shoulder, and they both stared down at the dropped pins across a map littered with notes on time and precise location. A cell tower ping that made its way through several areas, which the techs had narrowed down to following a particular highway from town to town. All of the points marking locations close by to where bodies had been found. A casino, a diner, a truck stop here and there with license plate recognition from the parking lot, painting a vague shape with long and large gaps between where the technology was not advanced enough.

Zoe searched the pins, willing the pattern to come into focus. She saw the lines, almost completely straight, allowing for the divergence of highways and curves around hills and water. It might as well have been drawn with a ruler if you ignored the roads and only looked at the stops. Though cell tower pings were not completely accurate, but rather gave a wider circle through which the cell must have passed, it was at least indicative of a deliberate movement across the country.

Not only that, but there were casinos at every waypoint. Zoe traced patterns and grids and curves between all of them, analyzing what the data told her until she could be absolutely sure that there was no other option.

There was only one direction in which Jimmy Sikes would go— that much was clear. Following it, Zoe saw a line as clear as day, cutting across the map as the crow flies, until she landed on the only place that made any sense.

He didn't know they were onto him, not yet. He wouldn't be looking to change his pattern in order to throw them off. They had him. She was willing to bet her career on the certainty that she knew where Jimmy Sikes was driving to.

"There," she said, placing her finger on the spot. "If we move now, then that is where we will find him."

Shelley peered down at the map. "The casino? How can you be sure?"

Zoe fought internally with the need to give her a plausible explanation, versus the need to keep all of that inside her own head. Now was hardly the time to reveal that she could read the numbers and patterns, even if she was intending to reveal that at all—which she was not.

"He likes to gamble," she said, at last. "Look, see? His first pickup point, just about five days ago, was at this casino, local to his sister's home. This was where it all began. He also passed by another casino at this point, here—though we are still waiting on the security footage from the interior, it seems likely that he went in, given his car's appearance in the parking lot. This is the next casino on his route. They are evenly spaced out—different counties, different owners. He goes to each one that he can reach without the fear of being recognized and thrown out. I would not be surprised if he is playing the house to earn money for his trip."

Shelley studied the three markers Zoe had pointed out, holding her blonde hair back over her shoulder so it wouldn't fall and obscure her view. She darted up a questioning glance, but seemed to think better of it from the determination on Zoe's face. After a pause, she nodded and straightened. "Okay, you're the boss. You've been doing this longer than me, so I guess you would know better than I can guess."

Zoe did not like the uncertainty in Shelley's tone, but there was nothing to be done about it now. They had to move. "Come on," she said. "We will head over now. Place a call to the casino management while we drive and tell them to be on the lookout for his vehicle and a man of his description. With any luck, we can catch him before he leaves."

CHAPTER TWELVE

The casino was over the Missouri border, just a stone's throw into Kansas. Not for the first time, Zoe was glad that FBI agents were not restricted by state lines.

Zoe watched as Shelley tapped on her phone screen, bringing up the vehicle's details again. A blue car, with the license plate that Zoe had spotted on the footage. Easy enough to spot—except for the fact that it was a popular and busy casino, and the parking lot was almost full.

They pulled up into a spot of their own, Zoe mentally cursing the inevitable draw of human behavior which left only the very furthest spaces still available. Then again, maybe it was a good thing, if it meant they could find the car on the way into the casino.

"I hope he's still here," Shelley muttered. She was fidgeting from foot to foot, fiddling with her necklace on its chain. Zoe sensed her nervous energy, a need to get moving that she also felt. The second car pulled up a few spots away, their backup pulled from the sheriff's crew.

They still hadn't heard about any bodies found overnight. Either he had been thrown off from his pattern for some reason, or he had made his kill such a successful one that the victim was still out there. Waiting. Zoe did not relish the thought, because every hour that passed meant further possible degradation of the crime scene and any evidence he may have mistakenly left behind.

Zoe did not share Shelley's hopes, for the simple reason that she had no doubts. He would be here. The records of his past few days had told her everything she needed to know. Jimmy Sikes was in that casino, and they were going to find him.

Not only that, but the security staff had called them back and told them of the car's presence. She had told them to watch the exit, make sure he was not allowed to leave. That should have meant that he was still inside.

Except for the call she had received only a couple of moments earlier, telling her that the security guard had been called over to a disturbance—and had lost sight of their man on the cameras. They were on alert to call as soon as they spotted him again, but in the meantime, they had to be sure that he was even still there.

They got out of the car, and Zoe nodded over at the other team. They had their orders already; silently, they fanned out, moving in pairs across the rows of vehicles, scanning plates and vehicle types. They were all armed, ready just in case the man resisted arrest, and on edge with the knowledge that it could go in that direction.

Zoe and Shelley moved down their row together, walking quickly, though not quickly enough to lose concentration. Time was of the essence. The quicker they brought him in, the less chance there was that he might somehow get away.

Zoe's eyes picked up different state plates, more Missouri and Kansas than any other. The tally ran on in her head without her bidding, the numbers appearing next to each vehicle. None of them the right one.

There was a crackle on the radio in Zoe's hand, and she lifted it to hear the message. *"We've got it. Far left row, mid-level. Vehicle is unoccupied."*

Zoe and Shelley looked up, the heads of the two other teams swinging in unison toward the furthest row in the lot. One hand waved in the air briefly, indicating the position of the car.

Zoe lifted the radio to her mouth. "We go in," she said. "You two stay with the vehicle in case of his return. If that happens, communicate with us immediately. The rest, with us."

They met at the entrance in a rush, all on the alert, wide eyes and stiff postures. There was a tension in the group, the kind of nervous energy triggered by the knowledge that the confrontation was soon to come.

"What do we do?" Shelley asked, yielding to Zoe's superior experience and knowledge. Moments like these reminded Zoe that her partner was not as seasoned as she sometimes came across.

"Two groups," Zoe said, looking around to check that everyone was listening. "Half with me, half with Special Agent Rose. I will go in the front entrance, the other team in the back. From there, we fan out. Leave one person behind at each exit. You all have your printouts?"

There were nods from all four of the local cops, and from Shelley.

"Take one last moment to study his face again before we enter," Zoe instructed them. "As soon as you see him, get on the radio and let us know his precise location. We will converge on him for arrest."

There were murmurs of assent and understanding all around as they each opened their phone screens or pulled out folded pieces of paper from their pockets to check Jimmy Sikes's image.

As they did, Zoe approached a member of the security staff belonging to the casino, flashing him her badge quickly in a way that concealed it from the view of passersby. After a few exchanged mutters, he took a spare radio from her hands and rushed it to his own control center.

Then they parted ways, three bodies in each direction, Shelley looking back at Zoe for a brief moment as if for reassurance. Zoe nodded to her, and Shelley turned to carry on.

Zoe steeled herself with a deep breath as she approached the entrance. The other team would need more time to get to the back of the building. They did not need to rush, not yet.

But that was not why she hesitated. She hesitated because she had been inside a casino before, and she knew what it did to her. What was about to happen to her mind.

She glanced quickly at the two cops beside her to check they were ready, and walked forward, pushing through the wide wooden doors and into noise and dim chaos.

The lighting was low, deliberately murky to hide the stains and to trick customers into losing track of the time of day. The room was wide and long, set up in different divisions, some beyond her view. The slot machines, some of them tall and showy, blocked almost everything on the right side. To the left were card tables and other games, and a bar stretching along it all that allowed patrons to walk up and get a drink whenever they wanted.

And, of course, the old casino classic: a meandering path which only ever led straight to the next gambling opportunity, rather than giving them a clear direction across the room.

Zoe took a breath, trying to keep her bearings. Trying not to let the numbers, the noise of machines and people and low lounge music, and the heady atmosphere of evening that almost immediately overwhelmed memories of the bright morning outside, get the better of her. They were everywhere she turned. She strode past a blackjack table, calculations appearing in her head as she saw all five sets of cards on public display and knew that the player seated to the right should hit, because there was an eighty percent chance of him getting the low-value card he needed to top up his score of sixteen.

On her other side, the glowing numbers above a slot machine declared a jumbo jackpot available across an interstate network, almost up to a record figure. The woman sitting there, playing a dollar at a time with resolute determination, must have known just as Zoe did that the machine was ripe to pop.

She looked ahead at the layout of the room, saw which slots were the ones that would pay out more often, placed in strategic locations to excite and encourage other gamblers. The harsh grating noise of a roulette ball rolling across the spinning wheel caught her attention, and she knew without having to wait for the result that the man with all of his chips on black fourteen was not going to get a win.

Zoe knew she would be able to clean up in a place like this. At the blackjack tables alone she could make a fortune, but the poker tables—to her left, four serious men in suits staring intently as the dealer flipped over an ace of clubs, giving the second player from the right around a seventy-five-point-five percent chance of getting a flush—there, she could take the lot of them.

Once, she almost had. Years ago, before she even entered the Bureau. She had been invited to a casino with a group of people she had known from work; acquaintances, really, since she had never been close enough to many people to call them friends. She had hit a few different games, always walking away with her chips at least doubled.

The first time, they laughed and clapped her on the back and congratulated her on her luck. The second time, she was apparently on a lucky streak.

By the fourth, they were giving her strange looks.

It was after her sixth game that she walked away, cashing in the chips so that she could leave and never have to spend leisure time with those people again. She had burned her bridges well enough. Once they looked at her like she was a freak, and even began to accuse her in whispers of cheating, she knew it was done.

There were things that she could not do, things that drew too much attention to her and the skills that she was trying to hide. Gambling was one of them. She had gone home after that and donated the money to a hospital, hoping that the benefit it gave the children's ward would stop the guilt she felt at using her power for something like that. It was wrong to cheat, and she had most definitely been cheating.

It wasn't that she wouldn't have liked to play again. It had been a fun night—very fun, until it started going sour. No, it was the risk and the guilt that stopped her. She had vowed that night never to gamble again, and she was not going to break that vow today.

Not that there was any time for something like that, when you were a special agent tasked with tracking down a mass murderer.

That knowledge did not mean that she could turn the numbers off. She tried to focus on faces and bodies, not cards and bets. There was no point in knowing that there was going to be a payout on the next spin of the roulette wheel, or which of the poker players was a shark and which genuinely had no idea how to bet. None of that would save the killer's next target.

Zoe followed the twists and turns of the path, alone now, her two shadows having slipped away—one to remain at the entrance and the other to her right, stalking through the maze of slots. She wound through the card tables, trying to look less like an agent and more like a seasoned gambler seeking the right game, though she hardly knew how to make the difference. So long as she looked at the faces, it was all right. But when she let her gaze dip to the tables to keep up appearances, the numbers flooded in, almost to the point of distracting her from her mission.

A movement caught her eye up ahead, and her gaze was drawn to another roulette table, this one served by an attractive blonde croupier. The woman was scraping chips toward winners, scooping the losing bets toward her, announcing the next game. A number of people were gathered around her, four—no, five—all with their attention on the betting grid.

And there, in the middle of them, with the side of his face toward her—Jimmy Sikes.

Zoe reached for her radio, lifting it to her face, but he was sharing a joke with another gambler and happened to look to the side and smile as Zoe moved toward him. He clocked the radio in her hand, her eyes fixed on him, and the laughter died in his throat. After a brief moment, perhaps half a second, he turned on his heel and pushed off at a dead run.

Zoe swore under her breath, pressing the call button. "Suspect identified. He is on foot, attempting escape from the card tables. Keep control of the exits." She trusted her own men, and the casino's own security staff, to handle that. So long as they were all in position, there was no chance he was getting away.

She dashed after him, seeing the cop out of the corner of her eye, moving out of the machines in her direction and beginning to speed up. Sikes was only a table ahead, but he had the advantage of the crowd, pushing through them and sending people scattering in surprise, resistant and forming new barriers when Zoe arrived a moment later.

He chanced a look behind him and saw how close she was, his eyes wide and wild. "Stop! FBI!" Zoe called out, giving him a chance to do the right thing.

They never did the right thing.

She was fumbling to unholster her gun while she ran, getting it into her hand, steadying it with the radio in the other. If he was armed, there was no telling what kind of move he might make. There was no way to know if he would resist them with violence.

"Stop and put your hands above your head!" she called out again, people scattering in front of her in response to her calls. Sikes zigged and zagged amongst the tables, looking over his shoulder with ragged gasps, panic written clear on his face.

He ran into a blackjack table, almost taking out the croupier as he body-slammed it, pushing with his arms until it flipped over and through the air, spending chips and cards flying. There was a crescendo so close in front of Zoe that she almost fell into it, and only the briefest pause before people were flooding forward, scrambling to pick up as many chips as they could hold, blocking her path.

"FBI! Get out of the way!" Zoe shouted desperately, but it had done the trick for Sikes. He was getting away, pulling out distance as she fought her way through the crowd. He had enough of an advantage now that she could see him getting away—and for good, if he managed to slip past their man at the door.

But he was running in a particular way, she could see now. He had been here for hours, most likely, making his way from station to station, playing different games, having a great time. He knew the layout of the room, at least better than she did. And there was a kind of method to his madness, a series of acute angles that jerked back and forth across the casino floor, ignoring the path entirely in favor of the fastest route toward the back of the room.

Zoe stopped moving and watched him. There was no sense in trying to shoot, not with this many civilians in the way. There was no way she could catch up with him now. But there were at least three other people in this casino who had a chance to stop him, and she could help with that.

She saw his path, traced like a line with a ruler in her mind's eye, a zigzag which was anything but random. He struck out left and right and skirted every other table, finding the clearest path to the door, even if it didn't seem to make sense to those who couldn't see it. The lines continued clearly right the way to the back of the room, which Zoe could now see as they entered the farthest part of the casino. Laid out in front of her from left to right, Zoe saw the lines overlaid on her view of the room in a literal sense, pointing her in the right direction.

And she could see Shelley, making her way toward him.

"Shelley," Zoe barked into the radio. "The end of the bar, to your left. Intercept him beside the third column."

Zoe watched Shelley hear the message, her head snapping around toward the bar. She noticed the column and headed toward it at a run, even as Zoe herself started moving again, following with her feet as well as her eyes.

One last row of tables to clear—

Jimmy Sikes dashed to the side, away from the cop that was approaching him, and skewed toward the bar, his feet taking around the fourth column in a row of them and beyond.

"Stop!" Shelley's voice, calling out, and then a crunching noise, like a body colliding with the floor.

Zoe's view was blocked by the third column—she could not see Shelley or Jimmy—but he had not emerged, and neither had Shelley. Zoe rounded the corner, opening up her view, and breathed a deep gasp of air in relief to see Shelley snapping handcuffs onto Jimmy's wrists with trained precision.

She arrived, a little out of breath and feeling the effects of the adrenaline that had flooded her system during the chase, as Shelley finished reading Jimmy his rights. The other cops converged upon them, taking Jimmy by the shoulders to march him back to the parking lot. Zoe breathed again, exchanging a grin and a secret fist-bump of success with Shelley.

"We got him, Z," Shelley said, laughing.

And Zoe wondered why she didn't quite feel so confident as she had a short while ago that they really did have their man.

CHAPTER THIRTEEN

Zoe slouched into a chair in the sheriff's office, her full attention on the screen of his computer. He had swiveled it around on his desk so that she could watch the video feed as, next door, Shelley sat down with Jimmy Sikes.

"It's probably not what you're used to," the sheriff said, by way of both gruff apology and defense of his precinct. "We don't quite have the budget that you all do up at the Bureau. No two-way mirrors and high-tech surveillance here. We don't have the space."

"That is fine," Zoe told him, nodding toward the screen. "I can see everything here."

"You sure she's fine in there on her own? I only mean, I gathered you were the senior agent."

"Special Agent Rose will handle it just fine," Zoe said, smiling. It was not for his reassurance or encouragement, but simply because she found his doubt amusing. "She has a reputation for interrogation. Just watch."

The man settled back into his own desk chair, the old leather creaking with his weight as they both watched in silence.

Shelley was already on the screen, sitting opposite Jimmy Sikes, whose handcuffs were threaded through a bar on the table to keep him in check. He had been watching her, chewing on one of his rough, dirty fingernails, for a good five minutes as she read through her files without saying a word. She calmly flicked through page after page, never so much as looking up to acknowledge him.

Zoe worried; not about Shelley, but about Sikes. He was heavier than she had wanted. The crime scenes had, she felt, indicated a

90

lighter man. Sikes had put some weight on since his details were last updated. Not only that but the way he chewed on his nails was—wrong, somehow. At odds with the careful fastidiousness told by the marks the killer never left behind.

Sikes was growing more fidgety, shifting his weight from side to side, spitting a chewed-up fingernail out on the floor. Shelley's technique was working, putting him off guard. He would have expected a fired-up shouting match, a grizzled old cop trying to intimidate him. The silence was not what he was used to—nor was the light and easy smile that Shelley flashed him from time to time as she continued reading.

Shelley finished looking through her files and glanced up, settling into a more comfortable and open posture. "Mr. Sikes," she said warmly. "Jimmy, if I may."

He stared at her, saying nothing, eyeing her out of one side of his head like a cornered dog.

"You've got quite the record, haven't you?" It was said with a smile, as if encouraging him to brag about his exploits rather than judging him.

"Served my time."

"What was that, Jimmy?"

"I said, I served my time. I'm out. You can't punish me for those no more."

"Well, we can, actually, Jimmy. Because you were released on probation, weren't you?" Shelley made a show of consulting her records, though Zoe knew she had already memorized them. "For aggravated assault, it says here. A violent crime."

Jimmy said nothing into the silence she left between them, only turning to spit another of his fingernails onto the floor. It hit the ground with a thud that was only audible to Zoe. The thud of truth. Their killer would never do that. Never leave DNA evidence behind.

"And because you were on probation, Jimmy, you weren't supposed to leave the state. Were you? And yet we have records that show you and your car moving all the way from your sister's home—Manda's home—down through Missouri and over here to Kansas. That's quite a journey, isn't it?"

Jimmy shifted, his eyes hitting the surface of the table between them. He was thinking something over, his gaze distant and unfocused. Zoe shook her head tightly. This was all wrong. Their killer was smart, calm, careful. He would have spoken, had some kind of cover already prepared. He would never have allowed Shelley to railroad him like this.

"You also failed to check in with your probation officer, and all in all, that means you're looking at going back inside for a violation. What a real shame. I'd like to see you rehabilitated, rather than facing more time behind bars." Shelley made a show of checking all the details in the file, then closed it and set it to one side. "Of course, I might be able to help you out there. Because that's not why we arrested you, is it?"

Jimmy's head swiveled up, his eyes squinting. "…Ain't it?"

Shelley smiled at him like they were best friends. "No, Jimmy. We arrested you because of the murders you committed this week."

Jimmy Sikes nearly fell out of his chair. "What? I never!"

Shelley tutted and shook her head. "Now, now. Don't lie to me, Jimmy. Not to me. I'm your best shot at getting a good deal with the judge, you know? I can help you figure something out—but only if you tell me the truth."

"I ain't killed nobody!" Jimmy shouted, shaking his head wildly. "I don't know what you think you got me on, but I just been having some fun. That's all. No killings."

And Zoe believed him completely. This was all a waste of time. Jimmy Sikes wasn't their man, and never had been. That was written in every slumped and careless angle of his body, the screwed-up lack of intelligence spread across his face, his word choices, his actions. Even the weight of his body.

She waited. Shelley would clear this up. They needed to be by the book, after all. If they weren't, people would wonder why Zoe had not followed up every lead available to her.

Shelley folded her arms on the table top, retaining her smile. "Well, Jimmy, why don't you tell me about the last few days, then? In your own words. Then we can sort out this silly misunderstanding."

Jimmy gasped for air, then shook his head just as wildly again. "I know what you cops are up to. No way. No. I ain't telling you a thing. You're gonna pin this on me, make me look stupid. I know cops."

Shelley sighed, resting her head on one hand. "I'm not a cop, Jimmy. I'm FBI. And all of this is being recorded. I'm not trying to trick you. I promise."

"I been here before." Jimmy shook his head. "No. Nope. I know this. You gonna try to pin it on me like that psycho ex of mine and her buddy the cop. I ain't speaking to you."

Shelley regarded him quietly, letting him cool down. "If you've got nothing to hide, you may as well tell me, Jimmy. If you have alibis, we can go check them out. See if you're on the cameras. There's always cameras. Even in here."

Jimmy looked up, frantically searching in the area that Shelley had pointed, until his eyes locked onto the lens. He stared right into it. Zoe shivered a little, feeling like their eyes were meeting even though of course he couldn't see her through it, the way that she could see him.

"So, you see, Jimmy, no one can make out like you said something you didn't say. It's all being recorded. And if I tried to trick you, I would lose my job."

Jimmy looked back at Shelley, sweating. "You're not gonna frame me?"

"You tell me what happened, and I'll tell you if you can go," Shelley said, layering meaning on the last words to make sure he got the point. "That's the only way you're getting out of here. And trust me, I don't want an innocent man sitting in here any more than you do."

Jimmy leaned back against his seat, his chain clinking and almost pulling him back when he tried to pull his arms too far. He sucked in a deep breath, then looked up at Shelley. "I was in the casino in Potawatomi. I hit a heater, you know? Got sat down opposite this green kid and took him for everything he brought with him, and his friend some besides."

"And when was this?"

"I guess like...four. Five days ago? Maybe four. I don't know exactly."

"You went to the casino from Manda's house?"

"Yeah."

Shelley checked the notes she'd written down from her call with Manda. "That was six days ago, Jimmy."

"Well, shit," he said, and laughed.

"So, you get this big win, right? A lot of money?" Shelley shifted her weight forward, giving him all of her attention.

"More'n I ever had." Jimmy nodded. "So I go out to the bar, and then I think, nah, I shouldn't be staying around here. The kid and his pals, the bouncers, maybe they got a thing against an ex-con winning big."

"So where did you go?"

"Got in my car and drove to the next bar. Just off the highway. Stayed there 'til closing time, then I slept a few hours in my back seat and drove to the next bar."

Shelley had been lifting her notes, checking through them, lining up his sightings with his story, but at this she paused and laid them down. "Are you telling me, Jimmy, that you've been drinking for the last five days straight?"

Jimmy shrugged. "Spent some of it at a couple of casinos, too. I got superstitious. Any time I had a good win, I moved on."

Shelley clicked the top of her pen, drawing out the nib. "I'm going to need you to give me the names and locations of these casinos and bars, Jimmy. You're doing great. We'll have you out of here in no time."

Zoe was already entering the name of the first bar into her phone, bringing up a search for the location—and the phone number. She walked out of the room and started to dial, watching from a window in the closed door as Shelley finished making notes and got up to leave the room.

"Hello? Yes, I would like to speak to your manager. My name is Special Agent Zoe Prime with the FBI," she said into the phone, catching Shelley's eye as she entered the corridor. "I am calling to request that you send over your surveillance footage from a few nights ago to help us in an investigation."

Between Shelley, Zoe, the sheriff, and his team, they tracked down all of the locations Jimmy said he had been. Though his times were a little off—no doubt distorted by the alcohol and the way time seemed to move differently inside casinos—several hours of trawling through emailed footage slowly ticked off his alibis.

He was visible in security camera reels during the estimated times of all of the murders.

Every single one.

Shelley slammed her notebook onto the desk in frustration. "We have to let him go. He's not the guy," she said.

"We'll still hand him over for the probation violation," the sheriff reminded her. "I'll go make some calls. They'll want to transfer him back to his home county."

He left Shelley and Zoe alone in their investigation room, the others having each filed out after checking their respective tapes. They were the only ones left, facing down once again the same position they had been in before tracking down Jimmy Sikes.

"We'll get him," Shelley said, wearily. "We will. This is just a little setback."

Zoe nodded. "I know we will. I wanted it to be before he took another victim. We have wasted precious hours with Sikes."

"How did you know where he was going to be?"

Zoe lifted her head at the abrupt question, ducking her eyes immediately when she saw that Shelley was watching her closely. "What do you mean?"

"You and I had the same data," Shelley said. "You knew as much as I did. But you managed to track him down to the casino, even though there was no way you could have known he would definitely be there. Then, when he tried to run—you knew where he would go. You directed me to the exact position where I could stop him."

Zoe said nothing. Technically, there had been no question. She could continue looking at the files in front of her in silence, her eyes roaming over words and pictures without seeing a thing.

"How did you know?" Shelley repeated.

Zoe felt something in her throat, a lump that threatened to swallow the easy, rehearsed words. Maybe she could admit it. Maybe Shelley would understand. She had been fairly understanding so far, and kind, and nice. Maybe this was the person that Zoe could confide in.

But the number of people in the world who knew about her synesthesia, the numbers and patterns that flew in front of her eyes wherever she looked, could be counted without needing all the fingers of one hand. And a secret that had been so closely guarded—the ability since childhood, and the diagnosis since she received it as a young adult—could not be so easily given away.

"It's just a combination of luck and experience," Zoe said, turning the page, still without reading a word. "Once you've been going for as long as I have, you'll be able to spot things a bit easier. Then you make your best guess, and hope you get it right."

There was something in the air now, something that hung so heavily over Zoe's neck that she was sure it must have gained visible physical manifestation. That Shelley was looking at her and seeing it, and knowing that she was not telling the whole truth.

"Just luck? That's how you knew he would dodge to the side, instead of staying on course to where the others were waiting?"

There was hard disbelief in Shelley's voice, a sternness and inflexibility that Zoe had heard many a time before. It was her mother's voice, her teacher's voice, the voices of the few friends she had had before they inevitably got weirded out and stopped calling her. It was the voice of everyone, eventually, when they stopped believing that she wasn't a freak.

You've got the devil in you, child.

The moments ticked away, Zoe's skin crawling beneath her shirt, sweat prickling from her pores. Shelley didn't believe her. Was this the moment where she had to confess? If she continued to pretend, would it be worse? Shelley could move on, find a new partner, and that would be bad enough. Zoe was getting used to her. Or she could bring it to their superiors.

Was now the time to tell her?

The landline phone rang, startling both of them with the abrupt way it cut into the stillness, slicing through their tension like a cheese wire. Shelley scrambled to answer it, dropping her papers on the desk and rolling her chair back toward the phone.

"Hello?... Yes?"

Zoe knew from Shelley's expression alone that it wasn't good news.

She hung up, her face blanching pale. "There's another body," she said. "Sheriff will take us there. It's not far. He's sending a team in with us."

Zoe felt her stomach sinking. They hadn't gotten away with missing him last night, after all. Even though she had expected it, it hit her like a ton of bricks. Another person had lost their life, because Zoe wasn't quick enough to save them.

"We wasted that time on Sikes," Shelley said, her tone hollow. She looked shell-shocked, like she was going to stand there for a long time without moving.

They couldn't afford that right now. They needed action. They needed to find the clues, stop it from happening yet again. Zoe grabbed her notepad, Styrofoam coffee cup, and bag and headed for the door. "Any details?"

"Just the location right now," Shelley said, shaking her head, seeming to pull herself out of her daze. Then she tossed her head to the side sharply, her tone changing. "Wait a second."

Shelley moved over to the map on the wall, grabbing a red pin and hunting the place names for a moment before pushing the pin into place.

"There?" Zoe asked, feeling confusion wash over her. "Are you sure?"

"That's what the sheriff said," Shelley confirmed.

Zoe took another look at the map, then turned to go, rushing out to the parking lot. This was wrong, all wrong. It was not far from their location, but still off from where she had predicted. How had she managed to mess it up?

The straight line was no longer intact—this pin swooping to the left and below the last pin, where the previous one had been to the right and below the original murder.

It wasn't a straight line.

Was it possible that it was a curve?

CHAPTER FOURTEEN

Zoe let Shelley take the driver's seat, as she sat by her side, thinking. Numbers and figures and curves. Could it really be true? Could she have been reading the signs wrong all this time?

The car threaded through back roads and along dirt trails, taking the shortest possible route at the sheriff's directions. He led the way in a battered police vehicle which had clearly seen better days, and he had no qualms about preserving the suspension or the tires. Being a rental, their car could not quite take the same level of punishment.

Zoe watched the scenery flash by the windows, clutching her seatbelt where it lay across her chest. She was always a little carsick as a passenger. Holding the belt away from her neck a touch helped.

They turned onto a highway. A large space of dirt and rocky ground ran alongside it, with trees growing beyond. It was evident that the work of human hands and machinery had cleared the space. No trees grew in straight, even lines in nature. Nature's patterns were circles, spirals. Could it be that their killer was taking inspiration there?

The presence of two marked police cars from the sheriff's station indicated their destination before the sheriff turned off, bringing his own vehicle to a stop beside them. Shelley audibly sighed in relief, loosening her grip on the steering wheel.

"Remind me never to get into a car with that man," she said, shaking her head as she pulled up to a gentle stop on the shoulder of the road, far out of the way of traffic.

Zoe jumped out of the car, anxious to get to the body. She wanted to see how this one had been left. It was their first opportunity to find a real body still in position, before the crime scene had been recorded and the victim taken away to the coroner's table. There were sure to be more clues here. Things that the investigators wouldn't have seen. Things that only Zoe could pick out.

A pair of white-faced middle-aged men, both dressed in the drab browns and greens of hunting gear, were leaning on the hood of one of the police cars. The sheriff made a beeline for them, and Zoe followed suit, glancing behind to check that Shelley was with her.

"Sheriff, these are the two hunters who found the body," the young deputy was saying. "They're a little shaken, but they didn't see much."

"You did not see another person in the woods?" Zoe asked sharply, cutting across the sheriff's mumbled reply.

The hunters looked at her wide-eyed, glancing over to the sheriff with confusion. With an impatient movement, Zoe took her badge from her pocket and flipped it open, allowing them to see for themselves that she was FBI.

"We didn't hear or see anything," one of the men said. "We were settled in the woods from the early hours, just sitting and waiting, all quiet like. We were listening for animals. Would've heard if something happened nearby."

"How did you discover the body?" Zoe asked.

"We were packing up to go home," the other explained, with a rueful smile. "Didn't catch a thing. The birds kept screaming. Thought they must have figured out we were there and weren't going to let nothing close to us without a warning. Usually they quiet down, but not these. So, after a few hours, we thought it best to go."

"That's when we saw the fox," the other put in. "Nose right to the ground, following something. He got spooked when he saw us and ran the other way, but the sun was up and we could see what he was looking at."

"Blood," the first hunter clarified. "All over the ground. A trail. Great spurts of it. Thought it had to be a wounded animal at first. But when we followed it, not far away, we found—"

The men both fell silent, looking at their feet, no doubt reliving what they had seen.

"Thank you for your help, gentlemen," Shelley said softly, as Zoe stalked away from them and into the trees. They had nothing more to tell her.

She did not have far to go. There were a series of flags and numbers laid out already, following a path across the sparse ground into the trees. Glancing back along their route, she could follow them to an access road which the sheriff had avoided taking them down, a point just far enough off the highway so as not to attract too much attention.

Zoe paused, heading back across the ground. She had a feeling that the access road was where it all started, and she wanted to do this chronologically. Lay the numbers out in a way that made sense.

By the access trail was a great spout of blood, a gush that must have come from the initial attack. A surge of adrenaline forcing the heart to beat faster, or perhaps movement as the woman pushed her killer away. This was not like the other murders—not like them at all. Zoe even had her doubts that this could be the one they were looking for.

Looking ahead, she noted the flags—each of them placed by a splash of blood. So many of them. This was a heavy wound. The spacing between them, several inches each time, told her of movement at speed. The regularity in distances between the flags, well, that was about the beat of a heart.

To leave such an obvious trail—right to a set of tire tracks which could be analyzed—was not like their man at all. Not only that, but the victim had not died where he found her. That was unusual in itself. Their man picked his victims carefully, and there was no chance for them to run or be discovered. They were left out in the open, with the confidence that he would be long gone before anyone had any idea of his presence.

No, Zoe could not see his hand here at all. She followed the blood marks, at times simple drips, at others larger pools. The calculations rushing by her eyes told her of a heart beating fast in panic, a dead run, a stumble here and there. Hands clasping the wound shut after a few steps had gone by, narrowing the range of blood flow to either side but not at all stopping it. Occasionally spraying out further droplets, creating a splatter pattern that was entirely unique.

Though the ground here was too dry and solid for clear footprints, she could ascertain the steps from the blood surges and pools. It came down heavier whenever the woman's feet landed, shaken loose by the impact. The woman's throat had been cut, sending the blood from high up, letting it gather into a wider-ranged pattern than it would have with a lower wound. The amount indicated an artery spill, no mere flesh wound. There was no wonder she was dead. This much gone already, and not even into the woods.

The blood was telling her things, almost too many to take in, in one moment. Distance—the woman was leaning forward as she ran, her body pitched, not quite as far off the ground as her neck would be if she stood straight. Spacing—speed, very fast, the run of someone who rightfully feared for her life. Two millimeters, three centimeters, two inches. All of those gaps told a story of desperation. And the loss of blood built a picture, too, pint by pint, Zoe counting in her head as she went. Nearly two before she even entered the woods.

Under the trees, the signs were clearer, though distorted in their own way by the effects of nature. The landscape became 3D, blood spots landing on tree trunks and exposed roots, rocks and low-growing leaves. It made no difference to the numbers. They still told her everything. Adjust for a two-inch raised mound of earth, calculate the distance from the ground to the woman's neck. Know that she was nowhere near upright. Her body collapsing downward as she moved forward. Three pints.

Zoe felt how the woman stumbled and fell but got up to run on, how she was almost crawling now, how she crept on as far as she could. The blood pattern was different here, coming down from a wound that was only a foot or less above the ground, less of a splash and more of a flow. No more crown marks of splatter. Four pints, then four and a half.

Then she had finally fallen, and Zoe was looking down at the obscenely wide open eyes of a dead girl, her neck gaping open like a second smile, her hands clutched in a death grip at the hem of her torn shirt.

Zoe dropped into a crouch, ignoring the deputy who was stationed over the body and even the presence of Shelley coming up behind her. She had to read these signs, figure out what they meant, see what everyone else was missing. Was this his work? Or not?

The girl lay in place on her back, but the blood patterns beside her told another story. She had moved, or been moved, an entire body width away; she had at first lain on her stomach, her hands clutched to her throat. The blood had spurted out of both sides of her neck where the wound could not be closed, forming two pools that must have spread out below her like macabre wings. From the width of the pools alone, combined with what she had already seen, Zoe knew it all added up to more blood than someone could live without. Another two pints in the pools alone. It had been the exsanguination that killed her.

Wings … Zoe peered closer, her eyes widening slowly as she realized what she was looking at. The symbolic association of the blood pools was that of a Rorschach blot, a pattern in something that was not really a pattern. It was almost perfectly symmetrical, just like one of those famous cards. That meant something—she knew it did, feeling it in the bottom of her gut. It would have meant something to him.

Where did that come from, that certainty? There had been no patterns to speak of at the crime scenes so far, had there? Zoe pushed that thought aside for the moment, focusing on the body in front of her. She had to determine, first, if this was really their killer.

The blood pattern, the thin cut to the throat which could have been done with razor-sharp wire, the choice of victim and location, the timing—this was him, after all. But something had gone wrong. She had slipped out of his grasp and managed to run, albeit not very far. She had almost escaped. He was usually in more control than that.

Zoe thought of the few remaining footsteps at Linda's crime scene, how the woman had been in sight of safety when he looped his wire around her throat and killed her. He was normally such a controlled killer. This was a break in his pattern, and it was not by design. The girl had fought him off. Zoe looked at her still, graying face with a rare burst of compassion, thinking of how hard she must have clung to life even to get this far.

The color told her something else: the time that had elapsed. He had attacked right within his normal window of time. When Zoe had been—what? Blurting out confessions about her difficult childhood, and feeling sorry for herself? Wasting those precious hours that could have saved this woman's life?

The coroner moved in, and Zoe stepped aside, allowing him to begin an initial assessment. Out here there were not the full, white-suited crime scene investigation teams of the inner city. It was just the coroner and his briefcase, and they were lucky to have that. Zoe barely needed to wait for him to finish—she knew exactly what they would tell her.

"What are you thinking?" Shelley asked, as Zoe approached. She had been waiting a distance away from the body, a vantage point from where she did not have to look at it—or smell it.

"Did you get a good look?" Zoe answered with a question of her own. She was beginning to be concerned that Shelley was a little too delicate—that she did not have the stomach for a crime scene. Besides which, she did not want to explain exactly what she had seen. The coroner could do that, and save Zoe explaining how she had seen it.

"Briefly." Shelley nodded. "It seems as though her throat was cut over there, on the access road, but she escaped and ran. She bled out here. I'm guessing, at least. I couldn't see any other wounds."

"Nor me. Everything was off for him this time. She nearly escaped, and though there appear to be some marks cleaned up near the body, he did not complete his usual total clean-up. I would imagine that forensics will be able to get more clues here than we ever have before."

"The tire tracks, and footprints, maybe."

Zoe nodded. "Not enough to identify his car or his person, not yet. But a step toward narrowing it down, evidence to present when we do catch him. It seems he is getting more desperate."

The coroner approached, rolling up a pair of clinical gloves and stuffing them back into his pocket. "I have done an initial investigation. Preliminary, of course, until I should have the chance to move her back to my office and take a better look. There I will be able to carry out the requisite tests and begin a more thorough investigation which ought to reveal more details than I am able to provide at this moment."

Zoe closed her eyes, fading the old man's voice out. He was the kind of person who would not use ten words to say something if a hundred could be used instead. The precise opposite of the kind of person that Zoe enjoyed conversing with. Instead, she thought about the scene, the way everything was slightly off-kilter.

Mentally, Zoe moved the red pin in the map in her head to the new location, a short distance away but still relevant. The road was the point where he had attempted the kill, and it was that which was significant, not the point of death. It moved the pin a little closer to her straight line, but not enough to make a difference. It had to be a curve.

"Where was the bruising?" Shelley asked, snapping Zoe back to attention.

The coroner indicated an area on his own body, over the ribs and stomach of his left side. "As I say, the bruising would have been inflicted postmortem, as there was very little blood left at this stage. That is all I can say from an initial investigation. I would say..."

"Anger," Zoe said, talking over him. "He was angry at her, for some reason."

"Perhaps because she ran," Shelley suggested.

"But she was dead already by the time he caught up with her," Zoe said. "He got his goal. So why was he so angry?"

Shelley spread her hands in a wordless gesture, the coroner beginning again his rambling monologue as if there had been no interruption.

Zoe's head was racing. There were more questions here than she had seen at any of the crime scenes—an irony, when what they needed desperately now were answers. Why had he chosen this road as his place, this random access road in the middle of a highway with nothing around it? Not a parking lot or a natural place to meet someone, like a footpath, as in his other crimes—why the change?

And why, if he had already achieved his goal of killing the woman, was he still angry enough to waste time kicking her—time that left him unable to finish covering his tracks?

Not only that, but something else kept catching at her mind. The Rorschach of the blood pools. The patterns. Why had that tugged at something in her mind, something that gave her a certainty that it was his work? If she could just figure out what it was that had linked that mental image with the other kill sites, she would have him.

The uncomfortable thought began to stir that maybe he, like her, could read the numbers. That maybe this was the work of someone with the devil's ability to see things no one else could.

Find the pattern, find the killer, Zoe told herself. And find him now—before he kills again.

Chapter Fifteen

Zoe sat at the side of one of the desks, getting a bird's-eye view of the investigation room. It was alive again, full of activity and of new sheets of paper joining the piles spread across the desks. There were so many files, now laid open to be read at a glance, something in them ready to give up their secrets if only she could look closely enough. The numbers she had already seen flashed before her eyes, just a distraction. They were not what mattered. It was the numbers Zoe had missed until now that she needed.

Zoe scanned over the reports in front of her, knowing that there was something here. Something they had all missed. If she could only get her teeth into it—

"We have a match for the tires," Shelley said, putting down the phone with a clatter as she spun her wheeled desk chair over to towards Zoe. "Sedan. Probably an older model, they think, judging by the width. The tread was fairly well-worn, so he's been on the road a bit. There's a few different manufacturers with sedans that use those tires, but it's a start."

Zoe nodded, pulling a sheet of paper from the fax machine. It baffled her that, in this day and age, the sheriff's team was still using a fax machine, but it was not for her to tell them how to renovate their office. "This is from the coroner. It is a photograph ... what is that?"

She tilted her head, analyzing the image. A splotch of green color on a white background. There was a standard rule to one side, indicating that it was less than a centimeter in both width and length. Other than that, the coroner had sent no information.

"Let me see?" Shelley held out her hand, and tilted her own head in a similar way. "Oh! It's a paint chip. I think. Let me call him and check."

Zoe ignored Shelley's call, filtering out her voice in the background. Paint chips and sedan models were good news for the investigation in general, but there was something else here. Something nagging at the back of her mind that she just hadn't quite figured out yet. Whatever it was, it could save the life of another woman— because the killer had not stopped or slowed down, and his pattern demanded another body tonight.

"It's a paint chip," Shelley confirmed, rolling back over. "The coroner says it was underneath one of her fingernails. Chances are good that it came from the killer's car."

Zoe tore her attention from the case files and got up, heading to their easel pad. "New profile, then," she said. "We are searching for an older model green sedan with out-of-state plates, driven by a male fitting the physical description we already worked up."

Shelley's face almost glowed with enthusiasm. "We're narrowing it down."

"It is still a wide net to cast," Zoe said thoughtfully, tapping the board pen against her lower lip. What wasn't she seeing here? "We should put out an APB on this description."

"On it!" Shelley jumped out of her seat and almost ran from the room, heading for the sheriff's office and his controls.

Her eagerness might have been annoying or off-putting, except for the fact that she was getting things done. Zoe had to admit to herself that she was happy to have another pair of hands and eyes on this. There were too many working parts, too many pieces of the puzzle missing, to do this by herself.

They were still heavily lacking in physical evidence, however. Identifying the car was one thing, and they had not truly been able to do that. There were still probably hundreds, if not thousands, of vehicles matching the description they had. Going through databases and tracking each of them down was not an option. By the time they had worked through the list, there would be bodies piled up in every state across the whole country.

Except that he wasn't targeting the whole country, was he? He was moving in a curve—a curve that only Zoe could figure out how to track. The numbers couldn't let her down, not this close to some kind of clue. She just had to keep looking.

Zoe glanced over crime scene photographs from each of the women, glazed eyes and open throats staring back at her. She could read all kinds of numbers in the frames. A twelve-inch skirt against an outfit that hovered only an inch above the ground. A 34D bust, a 40F, a 32B. Seventeen dollars stuffed into a phone case for safety that had not been taken. They told her something about the victims, but nothing at all about the killer.

In her bones, Zoe knew that they were right about his choice of victims. That it was the locations and the opportunity that mattered, not getting the exact right person into his grasp. She needed to stop looking at the women, as hard as that was when a blood-soaked body rested gray in full-frame under camera flash. She needed to look beyond them, at the place. The scene.

What wasn't she seeing?

Zoe began again, working through the photographs of the gas station. Frustratingly few of the images contained anything other than the body itself. In the background, she could catch the price of gas reflected in the windows, the three varieties of local newspapers on sale, count the yards between the victim and the front door. But there was nothing, nothing that told her who the killer was.

Something tugged at her memory, and Zoe frowned, shuffling through the photographs again. There was only one shot that contained a single, blue-colored piece of candy. But that wasn't right, was it? There had been more candy—much more. She remembered the colors scattered around her as she walked the scene.

She got up and walked down the corridor, to the small room down the hall where the local police photographer had set up his equipment. He was sitting in front of a large-screened Mac, the most modern piece of equipment in the whole place, and jumped when she thrust open the door without knocking.

"Can I help you, ma'am?" he asked nervously.

"The gas station crime scene," Zoe said, cutting to the chase. She did not appreciate it when other people delayed matters with small talk, and given that no one else appeared to enjoy it either, she wasn't sure why it was usually insisted upon. "Do you have any photographs of the candy that was scattered across the parking lot?"

The photographer stood, making his way to a filing cabinet at the side of the room and drawing out a slim plastic folder. He started to flip through printouts, each of them encased in a shiny plastic pouch for protection, until he found what he was looking for.

"Here," he said. "I grabbed one shot. I thought it was kind of whimsical, candy at a murder scene. Didn't seem to be any forensic value in it, though. Sheriff said it was probably dropped by a kid."

Zoe took the folder from his hands, studying the image closely. "Thank you," she said, turning to go back into the corridor.

"Those aren't really supposed to leave my room," the photographer said, but failed to follow up when she ignored him and continued walking.

Small-town protocol or not, there was something here. She could sense it. And if it was going to save someone's life, then she didn't give a damn about which room the folder was supposed to stay in.

Just one photograph. That underlined, more than anything else, the fact that no one else could see what she could see. Because this was it. She could feel it. This was something that they had all overlooked, but it was the key to the whole case.

Zoe sank back into her chair, her eyes running over and over the collection of candy on the floor. With this shot, taken from directly above and some distance up—perhaps on a step-ladder—she could see the pattern as it really looked. Because it was a pattern—just like everything else.

Most other people would have looked at that and seen a random scattering of candy. Something dropped by a child, maybe.

Meaningless. But if there was one thing that Zoe had learned over time, it was that nothing was ever meaningless. The hardy shrubs of Arizona grew a certain distance apart based on whatever nutrients they could find. Clouds formed on air currents, following pressure lines and forced by temperature and humidity. People moved in the same patterns day after day, life after life, driven by pre-ordained social assumptions and genetics.

And the candy had fallen into near-perfect vertices of a convex polyhedron. All you had to do was connect the dots to see the straight lines drawn between each one. They were plain to see, once you knew how to look.

Almost anyone would have dismissed this as random trash, something to be cleared up and thrown away. But he hadn't. He had cleaned away everything else, the footprints, any traces of his presence. But he had left those dropped pieces of candy behind, scrupulously avoiding them, letting them stay where they fell.

There was a moment of doubt in her mind, but in truth it was not doubt that she was wrong. She knew she had to be right. The doubt came from fear, fear that she had something in common with a brutal killer. A serial killer—one who treated human lives like pieces of scattered candy. Something disposable, used only for the creation of a pattern.

A fear that she could turn out to be the same. The devil was in her, her mother had said.

Zoe knew she wasn't an evil killer—even if she had difficulty connecting with other people, she still saw them as humans. The fear came from outside herself, from her mother's superstitions and the need to hide who she really was.

But fear or no fear, she could not deny what she was seeing in front of her. All of the pieces clicked into place, a complete picture now, and though they might be rearranged she could not imagine them telling any other story.

Now Zoe knew who their killer was. He was like her. He saw things the way that she did. He looked at those scattered pieces of candy and saw a divine signal that he was on the right track. He looked at the Rorschach pattern of wings left by a neck wound and it encouraged him to go on.

He wasn't just making a random curve driven by necessity. He was forming a pattern.

And now that she knew him, she could catch him. She could make him stop.

The only question was whether she could do it before he took another life.

Zoe came back to herself, realizing that she had been staring off into the distance, thinking for quite some time. She was seeing everything from a new perspective. Everything had changed. He thought the same way that she thought—and Zoe knew how she thought better than anyone else.

Shelley had come back into the room to sit quietly looking through the files, but Zoe barely noticed that she was there. She was too focused, and her mind was swirling.

Zoe grabbed and hastily assembled each of the victim files in order, taking both the crime scene notes, the coroners' reports for all but the latest body, and the photograph that best showed the full scene. Seeing them all side by side like this, it was clearer than ever that there was a connection. The gaping second mouths across the throats, all the same width and depth to within a millimeter, the pressure applied to precisely the same degree each time.

All the work of the same two hands. Hands that even now were clasping a steering wheel, driving him to the destination where he would meet his next victim. Zoe eyed the map on the wall, took in the curve. Saw the towns that were potentially in its path. She focused in on a particular area, the zone where the curve was likely to continue—a rural town, just a few buildings, a waypoint on the road.

No one was going to die there tonight. Not if she could do anything about it.

A deputy came and knocked on the door of the investigation room, hesitating with a brown paper bag in his hand.

"Come in," Shelley said, offering him a smile. "Is that lunch?"

"The sheriff said I should bring you something," he said, pausing again before stepping into the room, as if crossing a forbidden line. "I didn't know what you liked, so I got a few different sandwiches. And some pastries, too."

"That's very kind." Shelley smiled, taking the bag from him.

"Is it lunchtime?" Zoe asked, looking up at the old-fashioned clock mounted on the wall. Time was running away from them. She could count the number of hours before he would attempt to kill again on one hand. Certainly before midnight, there would be another body—unless she could find him first.

Zoe thanked the deputy and reached indiscriminately for a sandwich, not caring which one she lifted out. It turned out to be grilled cheese and tomato, a fact which she barely registered except to note the half-inch thickness of the bread, the fact that the slices comprised only two-thirds of a tomato, and the uneven flare of butter along each side of the interior. Whatever it was, to a brain which needed fuel, it was delicious.

The files in front of her took her attention, the numbers even clearer now than they were before. She saw at a glance their heights, their ages, the salary they earned each year, the year in which they graduated from high school (or failed to do so), the number of dependents they had, the length of their hair in millimeters. None of it provided any kind of link or pattern.

Zoe was coming up short, but it was not necessarily a bad thing. This was a sign that she was on the right track. Ruling out a link between the victims meant that her instinct was correct, and the location was the thing. She was now more sure of that than ever. The extra twenty minutes to be certain was worth it—and the evidence was in the last victim, the young woman they had identified as Rubie.

Why would the killer be so angry with the woman who ran from him that he would kick her, even after death? It didn't make sense—not if you couldn't see the way he thought. If you looked at it from the perspective of any other person, you might say that he was just frustrated, or dumb, or petty enough to delight in kicking a dead body. None of which was borne out by the other crime scenes.

Zoe put herself in his shoes. If she was the killer, what would she be so angry about? What on earth would make her feel mad about getting her way?

Unless, of course, she hadn't entirely gotten her way.

That had to be it. And just like that, Zoe knew.

The answer was a simple one. Not because she had fought back—they all had, to some degree that they were able, even if it was just to flail around and gasp for air. It was not simply because she had run from him, or fear that she would not die—because she had died, by the time he found her in the woods.

No, it was because she had ruined his pattern. Zoe could see that now, as clear as the bright sunlight streaming in through the windows in the hall outside, casting a square of glowing yellow on the far wall that encapsulated their easel board and made it almost impossible to read the profile written on it.

Zoe didn't need the profile anymore. She knew what she was looking at now.

A man who lived for the patterns, lived and died by them. Or rather, killed by them. The pattern was important to him above anything. Which meant that the curve on the map was not just a curve—it was a message.

A message that Zoe was now determined to understand.

The phone on the wall burst into a shrill ring, scattering her thoughts. Shelley got up to answer it without being asked, which was another reason why Zoe was beginning to like her very much.

"Really?"

Something in Shelley's tone, the sharpness of it, made Zoe look up and pay attention.

"When was this? ... And you've just flagged up the match in the system now? Right, yes. If you could fax everything over as soon as possible. Thank you."

She put the phone back into the wall holder, then turned to Zoe with wide eyes. "There's another one. Five days ago, but the local PD only just put the data into the system and saw the match with our cases. Looks like it might have been his first kill."

Zoe shot out of her seat, heading to the map pinned up on the wall. "Where?"

There was only one question that mattered now. The who was irrelevant. The how was obvious—murder by garrote, otherwise it would never have flagged up as a match. The why was becoming clearer at every step they took.

It was the where that could unlock the whole thing.

Shelley ran to the fax machine, grabbing out the first piece of paper it was hastily spewing. She scanned the page hastily, shouting out a town name as soon as she found it.

Zoe scanned the map, looking for something along the straight line or even the gentle curve that she now knew it was. Where was this town? She searched names again and again, not seeing it, wondering where it could possibly be.

She stepped back, gesturing for the piece of paper, taking it from Shelley's hands and examining it herself. The name of the place was right. So then, why wasn't it where it was supposed to be?

Zoe looked up, and by chance her eyes dragged over another part of the map as she oriented herself, and the name jumped out at her. *There.* But not at all where she had expected it to be. It was way off to the side, far above the latest pin. Zoe pushed the new marker into the wall and then stood back again, taking it all in.

And, oh, how stupid she felt at that moment, now with all of the clues in her possession.

What she had at first mistaken for a straight line with clumsy deviations, and then for a curve, was in fact neither of those things. The turn was too steep to be accurately described as a curve. It was a shape instead, a shape that had yet to be completed.

But it was too steep, again, for it to be a circle. If the data points ever did meet in a closed loop, it would have been squished and off-centered, a strange misshapen thing. The pattern mattered far too much to the killer for him to make that kind of mistake. No, it was not a circle.

It was a spiral—or it was going to be, once he finished it.

A little squished, a little strained, but a spiral.

How could she have missed this for so long? Rubie wouldn't have needed to die if Zoe had worked out that the next point would be somewhere along that highway. They could have stationed cars and dogs and helicopters. They could have caught him, even if his spiral was too deviant from a truly composed shape to be completely accurate with her estimations.

But did that fit with what she was thinking? If he was focused on the pattern, would he really allow it to be so imperfect? That didn't seem to sit right with Zoe.

The victims didn't matter, and they never had. Their killer was just picking someone in the right place at the right time—for his purposes, at least—and making them into a pin on a map. If the victims didn't matter, and the killer was so angry at his latest victim for running, then—

Zoe took the pin out of the woods, where the body had been found, and moved it back to the very entrance of the access road. The point where he had actually attacked.

"Shelley, was the victim found dead in the place where the attack happened?" she asked, urgency in her voice.

Shelley flipped through the other pages that the fax machine was still spitting out, frowning. "Hold on, let me...Um...No, it doesn't seem like it. The man was found outside a farmhouse—wait, man? That breaks the pattern."

"No, it doesn't," Zoe said impatiently. "Come on. Where was he attacked?"

"On the grounds of the farm." Shelley stepped forward, placing her finger on the map. "Here. It looks like he ran."

Zoe moved the red pin, just a small degree. But when she had done that, the spiral was neater, more composed, more aligned with what she might have expected. It turned out that they had been looking at it wrong from the very beginning. It was not the sites where bodies were recovered that mattered. It was where the attacks took place—the specific and precise locations where the killer wanted them to be.

The phone rang again, somewhere distantly at the range of Zoe's attention. She ignored it, letting Shelley take care of it. That was not important right now. What was important was the pattern.

He had not waited for the gas station attendant to round a corner because he wanted to distract her, or give her false hope, or because it was all a game. It had been there because it had to be there, otherwise his spiral would not work.

In fact, looking at it now, Zoe would call it a perfect spiral. Nothing was a mistake, and there was no deviation. This was a perfect spiral of the kind that was seen everywhere in nature, a Fibonacci spiral, the spacing decreasing in precise ratios until it reached an end point.

That meant two things. The first was heartening: it was that there was going to be an end to the murders.

The second was less so.

It was that there were three more murders to come before the spiral was complete.

CHAPTER SIXTEEN

Zoe waited for Shelley to finish her call, tying up loose ends, discussing the latest body. All kinds of thoughts raced through Zoe's mind, calculations and flashes of the prior crime scenes, things linking up and making so much more sense. She saw distances between scenes, diminishing in distance each time, painting the picture that she should have seen all along.

Shelley put the phone back in its cradle and moved back to the fax machine, seemingly unaware of the epiphany that had overwhelmed Zoe for the long minutes since she had seen it.

"I have it," Zoe breathed at last to get her attention, staring at the map in a mixture of wonder and horror. "I know where he is going to strike next."

"What?" Shelley looked up, abandoning her attempt to marshal all of the pieces of paper that had finally stopped coming through the fax machine. "But I didn't even tell you the rest of the details yet. What if this isn't one of his?"

"It is his," Zoe said.

"But it's a man—that breaks his profile. Most killers don't break gender or race lines. They target one thing and one thing only."

"Shelley." Zoe turned, gestured to the chairs. "I know they tell you all of that stuff in training. The statistics, the general rules that killers move by. But believe me—this is his. I can see his pattern now. Let me explain it."

Shelley sat, her eyes wide, her arms folded on the desk in front of her. She looked totally nonplussed, though whether at the fact that Zoe finally had the answers or at the way she had spoken to her, Zoe couldn't tell.

"We are dealing with a schizophrenic," Zoe began, standing in front of her, presentation-style. "I believe he will have a precise form of schizophrenia known as apophenia."

Shelley opened her notebook and wrote that down. "What does apophenia mean?"

"An apophenic is someone who is obsessed with patterns. When they are suffering from a delusional episode, they may feel that the patterns are speaking to them or that they are a sign left by a higher power. They see two things and create a connection between them, when there really is nothing there to see."

"So, for example…" Shelley chewed on the end of her pen, frowning as she thought. "If I was saying out loud that I didn't know what to do with my life, and I saw an advertising billboard immediately afterward that said 'Visit Nashville,' I would think that God was telling me to go to Nashville."

"Good example. Except that with schizophrenics, this can go much further. They latch onto signs and patterns, and they become truly obsessed. Their lives become dedicated to these patterns. They might stand on a train track and wait for an encroaching train because the pattern told them to."

"Or they might kill someone." Shelley's voice was soft and quiet.

Zoe paused, giving Shelley a moment's respectful silence as she had noted others doing in serious situations, then nodded. "We thought for all of this time that he was cleaning up his crime scenes to prevent us from tracing him, that he was an accomplished and educated killer, someone who had enough knowhow to stop us from catching him. If I am right, that may well have been simply a lucky side effect of his need to keep the pattern intact. He erases himself, any marks left behind that could distort the pattern. That is all."

"So, you know what his pattern is?"

"I do." Zoe moved over to the map, indicating the red pins. "Look. If you follow them around in chronological order, we clearly have the beginnings of a spiral. A perfect spiral, in fact, modeled on the Fibonacci spiral."

Shelley furrowed her brow. "That's...hold on, let me try and remember. Something to do with nature, ratios in nature?"

"Correct. It is a series of numbers which define the ratios of many naturally occurring things. We see it in the shells of snails, the way petals grow on flowers, weather formations such as hurricanes. Almost everything, actually. To an apophenic, it might as well be catnip. The perfect obsession, because it really is everywhere."

"But that means he has to keep killing, in order to finish the spiral."

Zoe pulled out three new pins, pushing them into the precise points on the map where the spiral should be completed. "Three times. One of which will be tonight."

"And those are the locations." Shelley slipped her pen into her mouth, chewing the end of it. Her eyes were flicking backward and forward between Zoe and the map, as if she were trying to find some secret hidden message of her own.

"We need to put out alerts, and get a team together to stake out tonight's location."

"Wait," Shelley said, shaking her head. "Are you...sure about this? I mean, you've moved some of the pins. And we've got no real clue about who the killer is, let alone whether or not he has any psychological problems. We're going to mobilize half a state's worth of law enforcement professionals on one location, based on the fact that there may be a spiral pattern? What if he's just circling around his home, going out to a new location every night and getting closer because he's getting cockier?"

Zoe had to admit, the way Shelley described it made sense. This wasn't a television show, when the arrogant yet genius agent could pull all of the Bureau's resources to track down a simple hunch. They needed proof, tangible evidence, and failing that, a strong sense of possibility. Much stronger than guesswork.

But it wasn't guesswork. It was just hard to convince someone of that when you weren't able to explain to them exactly how you knew what you knew.

"He would still move in the same direction."

Shelley shrugged, her shoulders lifting up and down as if weighted by a heavy burden. "I'm sorry, Z. I know you have more experience than me. But I just don't understand how you got from that map to being so sure about where he'll strike next. Maybe you can explain it to me? It might help me get better at this. Next time, I might be able to spot the pattern."

Zoe shook her head sharply. There was no point. Even if she explained every little thing that she could see, clear as day on the map, Shelley would never be able to get there on her own. Zoe couldn't teach the kind of skill that she had. It wasn't born of experience. It was something she could just do—had been able to do since she was able to think.

"I cannot explain it any clearer than I already have."

A frown creased Shelley's features, and Zoe braced herself. Here it came. The inevitable breaking point of any partnership she had ever had since joining the FBI. Shelley would get mad. She would argue and try to discourage Zoe from following the right path. When Zoe turned out to be right, she would accuse her of somehow colluding with the murderer. Of being involved in some way herself, or hiding evidence that would have allowed anyone else to come to the same conclusion.

She would shout and scream, call their boss and ask for a transfer. And just like that, Zoe would be given a new partner again.

It was a shame. She had been starting to really like Shelley. They had gotten along all right until now, hadn't they? But no matter how Zoe tried to interact with her partners, give them what they seemed to want, it always turned out the same. She didn't know how to calm their suspicions and stop the shouting. The truth wouldn't cut it.

Might as well get it over with. Zoe picked up a ruler and pen and began to draw straight lines that intersected between all of the red pushpins on the map. One by one she connected them, laying ink over the lines that were already visible in her mind. Then she put down the ruler and drew a freehand spiral that connected line to line, as perfect a Fibonacci as she could do without mathematical drawing devices.

"Can you see it now?" she asked, pushing three red pins into the last remaining locations. "Look. I am right about this. You have to trust me."

Zoe turned and met Shelley's gaze. The other woman's face was set not in the anger or frustration that she expected, but more of an awed confusion. She could see the pattern, that much was clear. But she still didn't understand how Zoe had gotten there, and she never would.

"We have the same data, don't we?" Shelley asked, softly. "I can't see it in all of this. I can see it on the map now, but I don't know how you got there. How did you know that those pins would form a perfect shape with those lines?"

"I am not hiding any information from you," Zoe snapped. She was tired of this already, wanted it over. Wanted Shelley to just shut up and let them alert the local authorities, get people in place for a stakeout. They were wasting valuable time. "We have to act now. Do not argue with me."

Shelley stood, and Zoe almost flinched, ready for the confrontation to ramp up. She could not show weakness, not now. She had to maintain the confidence, use her position as the senior agent. It went against everything she told herself to do in normal situations, but lives were at stake. She clamped her lips together in a firm, straight line, determined not to bend.

Shelley moved in front of her, sat down on the edge of the table. "Z...it's okay," she said. "I'm not trying to fight with you. I just want to understand."

Zoe said nothing. Inside, however, her resolve flickered. No one had ever reacted this way. Whenever she revealed any hint of her gift—or her curse, whichever it was—she was treated with suspicion and accusation. Not this. Not the open, soft expression Shelley was giving her, the quiet voice, the words of encouragement.

"You can see something I can't, somehow, can't you?" Shelley took a breath, then reached out to touch Zoe's arm. "I was warned by the Chief that you'd had a lot of different partners before. That they called you things—made accusations. I'm not here to do that. You can tell me, and I'm not going to demand a transfer. I like working with you."

Zoe hesitated, looking down at where Shelley's warm hand rested on her arm. A gesture of comfort. There was something motherly about it. Not that Zoe had real experience of how a mother was supposed to act, but she could guess that this would be it. Like the mothers on television in old sitcoms, reaching out an olive branch to their confused and frustrated teenagers.

Maybe it was the comparison, making her feel young and defenseless again. Maybe it was just the fact that Shelley sounded genuine, as if she really would accept Zoe, warts and all. Or maybe it was simply the almost-symmetrical lines on her face, the reassuring angles and axes that Zoe saw in numbers all over her skin. But whatever it was, something made Zoe open her mouth and speak.

"I have a condition," she began. "It means that I see things … differently."

"Differently, how? Like … apophenia?" From any other person, it might have sounded like an accusation. Zoe would have expected them to want to send her away to a psych ward, get her taken out of the Bureau. But Shelley was only seeking to understand, without judgment.

"Not quite. The patterns I see are—real. It is not just patterns, though they are a part of it. I see the world in numbers. I can tell you the distance between markers on the map without measuring it, the degree of angles between them. From there, the pattern follows."

"What else can you see?" Shelley's tone was one of wonder and excitement. Positive emotions, Zoe felt sure. Not the negativity she usually heard. Even still, she braced herself for a sudden switch, a smile transformed into anger and resentment. Even as she carried on.

"Everything," she said, gesturing around helplessly. It was difficult to explain it all fully to someone who had never experienced it. Like trying to explain what it was like to see in color to someone who only saw black and white. "I know the number of millimeters that prevent your face from being exactly symmetrical. I count the chairs and desks in the briefing room the moment I enter, instantly. I can read footprints in the sand and know the height, weight, and running pace of the suspect. A knife wound tells me the dimensions of the blade. I see the numbers in everything."

Shelley was silent for a moment, digesting it all. Zoe wanted to close her eyes. This was it—the moment when Shelley turned on her. It was coming now, the calm before the storm.

"Wow," Shelley breathed. "Z, that's amazing. You have a serious gift."

Zoe blinked.

"I mean, this is amazing. No wonder you're so good at catching people. With such a good solve rate, I wondered how you couldn't keep partners. I thought you had to be arrogant or something, but this?" Shelley shook her head, a smile bursting and lighting up her face. "With a gift like this, you can do so much. Save so many people."

Zoe reached for a chair and sat down, winded. "You are not angry with me?"

Shelley half-laughed, reaching to touch her arm again. "No, Z. Why would I be angry?" A moment passed, and there was a flicker across Shelley's expression, something that Zoe could not read. "Oh. Because—because you've been made to feel like you're ... different? In a bad way?"

Zoe studied her own hands, lowering her head. "My mother said it was a gift from the devil."

"That isn't true," Shelley said. "I know it isn't. Jesus, no wonder you don't like Christians. I mean—excuse my word choice."

Zoe had to laugh, even if it was a small and quiet one.

The tension in the room was gone, and Shelley was looking up at the map with a renewed understanding. "We have to get on this right away," she said. "You're the only person who can possibly understand how the killer thinks. Once we explain it at the briefing, everyone will be on board."

Zoe's head snapped up sharply. "You cannot tell anyone," she said. "Not about me. It is between us, as partners. No one else can know."

Shelley hesitated, but caught Zoe's eye and nodded.

"Promise me," Zoe said.

Shelley wet her lips before answering. "I promise. It will take some thought to present this in a way that makes sense without people knowing what you can see, but I won't say anything. So long as you promise me something, too."

"What is it?"

"Not to keep anything from me. If you can see something, tell me," Shelley said. She shook her head, although there was still a smile on her face. "I just thought about the guy we caught the other day, in the desert. How you knew where he was going to be, and everyone thought you were wrong. You could see it, couldn't you?"

"Plain as day." Zoe took a deep breath. "All right. I promise that I will tell you everything from now on, in relation to our investigations."

The clarification was necessary. Zoe didn't want to promise to tell Shelley literally *everything*. That would have been too much.

"Shake on it, partner?" Shelley held out her hand with a twinkle in her eyes.

Zoe shook, and the deal was done.

"Now, let's get some more precise maps, and we can start figuring out the exact coordinates where we need to keep watch," Shelley said, getting up and moving toward the computer already.

Zoe finished the last line over an hour later, taking her ruler away and examining her handiwork. It was clean and precise, just the way she needed it to be. Not a single mistake. Zoe had always been good at precision. It wasn't so hard, when you could already see the lines and angles and calculations laid out on the page for you, before you put them down in ink.

"Right," Shelley said, standing back. "They're all lined up exactly."

They stood for a moment to take in the maps of the three Midwest states that the killer had already targeted, placed in precise relation to one another across all of the tables they had been able to find and push together. These maps were much clearer. They were able to differentiate more clearly the precise locations of each kill, rather than a wider point that took in other buildings and roads.

Zoe lifted the sheets of tracing paper she had managed to find in the desk of one of the sheriff's deputies, who was apparently a bit of a craft enthusiast. Over it, Zoe had been drawing a perfect grid of squares with her trusty ruler, while Shelley printed and stuck the map pages together. Now, she laid the grid over the top of the map, making sure that the points each lined up with the murder locations.

She took a pen in a different color and drew the spiral again, connecting the kill sites in chronological order. She did not really need the grid to know where the line had to flow, but it was there for Shelley's benefit.

"Here, we can see that our killer is operating in a reverse Fibonacci spiral, starting from the furthest point and working his way down," Zoe said as she drew. "Now, watch. The spiral moves across the grid in a predictable manner, so we can work out precisely where it will finish. It passes through these points—here, here, and here."

Zoe drew a circle around each of the last three locations needed to finish the job.

"He started wide to try and avoid running into suspicion for as long as possible," Shelley guessed, her fingers tracing the first murder sites. "With Kansas, Nebraska, and Missouri involved, it was going to take a while for the states to work together. And it did. Four murders before we even got here, and one since. He must have suspected that we would track him down quickly once we saw that the murders were all connected."

"Even though he is careful to remove traces of himself, and even though the locations are free from surveillance, there was always a chance that he would be seen in some way," Zoe agreed. "His car could have been identified on the road. Spreading wide at the beginning and then focusing down was the best way to give himself a chance of getting it all done."

"But now he will be operating in a much smaller area. Which is good news for us."

"And the locations will be even more precise. We will be able to narrow it down perfectly."

Shelley pressed the tracing paper down, ensuring she could read through it. "The next kill site is a roadside attraction...what does that say? I think some kind of fair. Then we have a little town circled—oh, no, that one will be so much easier for him! And then it looks like the last one is just...open ground? Nothing there in particular."

Zoe followed Shelley's discoveries, thinking. "We only have to stop him once. We stake out the fair tonight. It is not about where the body will be left, but where the actual killing will be done. We have to catch him in the act."

"That's not going to be easy," Shelley said, playing with her pendant, worrying it back and forth around her neck.

"We still have to try," Zoe said. "Get him tonight, before he strikes the town. I will call the Kansas state police chief and organize a briefing. We have to mobilize now."

Zoe watched the assembled twenty-four men and women with a twitchy feeling of anticipation. Her mind was working in overdrive, scanning them for details. The full two centimeters that one trooper's moustache grew over the edge of his lips. The youngest trooper in the room, at twenty-one, and the oldest easily in his mid-forties. The way that societal hierarchy had granted the chief of police a chair at the front of the room in the very center, while those keen for promotions ensured to sit as close to him as possible.

"We believe that the killer will be targeting this location next: the Kansas Giant Dinosaur Fair," Shelley announced, standing in front of the map they had blown up for the briefing. "I'm sure those of you who are local are familiar with it, but in summary, it's a permanent roadside attraction with around twenty giant dinosaur statues. Around these are a number of carnival games, food stalls, memorabilia stands, and so forth."

"The bad news," Zoe said, taking over, "is that tonight is a special Family Night event. The fair will be running a number of special features, as well as a discounted entry fee for groups of three or more. This means there will likely be a high number of people in attendance, making our jobs that much harder."

"Why don't we shut down the fair?" one of the local troopers asked, raising his hand.

"We do not want to spook him," Zoe replied. "Remember that he will not just be planning to strike tonight in this location, but also at other locations in the future, judging by his track record thus far. If we stop him from killing tonight, we save a life. But if we catch him tonight, we stop him from killing ever again."

Shelley took over. "We have a little information to go on, which should make it easier to track down our man. We'll focus on the parking lot, as we know what kind of car we're looking for. It's an older-model green sedan, with likely with out-of-state license plates. To be sure, we will be tracking all sedans fitting the description and watching the drivers. We are looking for a male suspect, likely traveling alone."

"What if he's changed his car?" This time from another trooper.

"We have no reason to believe he knows we have identified his car," Shelley said. "Besides which, that's our only lead. We don't know what he looks like in any particular, even down to his race. We have no living witnesses. We have to focus on the car by dint of having nothing else to go on."

"How do you want us deployed?" asked the chief of police.

"We will need to avoid suspicion," Zoe said, moving the map aside to show a diagram of the attraction and its parking lot. "This man is a habitual killer, which means he will kill again if he is not stopped tonight. We cannot risk spooking him. If he runs, there is no guarantee that we will find him again. Myself, Special Agent Rose, and eight further state troopers will take the parking lot, in plain clothes. Ten of you will walk through the fair and blend with the rest of the attendees, looking for any suspicious behavior. The rest of you will wait in unmarked cars at these locations, here and here, further down the road. Your task will be to form a cordon if he manages to leave the parking lot."

"Any questions?" Shelley scanned the assembled police, her gaze moving from face to face.

One arm shot up in the back.

"I went to the Giant Dinosaur Fair last year. It's open all day long. How do we know he isn't already there?"

Zoe looked at Shelley, who looked back.

"We had best get moving," Zoe said, grabbing her jacket from the back of the briefing room. "Chief, please alert your contacts at the fair as we drive. Get them searching now. We will need to sweep the parking lot for existing cars when we arrive. He could already be there—may already have his victim. We move fast, and we move now."

CHAPTER SEVENTEEN

The air was cold on Zoe's face and hands, but not so chill that it had deterred the crowds. Judging by the full parking lot, it was obviously a popular event with locals.

Above the lines of cars already parked, haphazardly in spaces painted on the ground, the fence stretched, encircling the whole fair. No entry without a ticket, and only one single ticketing gate. Every man, woman, and child who attended had to enter through that space. That, at least, would make it a little easier to watch the flow of people through the parking lot.

Higher still, when Zoe tilted her head, she saw the dinosaurs. Crude yet imposing statues, their mouths perennially bared to the elements, exposing sharp teeth. A Tyrannosaurus Rex stood about a foot taller than a Velociraptor, which was patently ridiculous; in life the T. Rex ought to have been at least three and a half times larger in scale.

"Pair off," Zoe said, nodding to the troopers arranged in a loose group around her. "We do not risk attracting attention. You two, stand by the entrance as if you are waiting for friends. Use your radios immediately if you see a green sedan entering the lot. Everyone else, stroll together, and check the plates in your assigned sections. Carefully."

With her last word of warning, the troopers—along with Shelley—began to move out. They had divided the vast parking lot into segments, each of them checking plates on a set section of cars. Security at the fair was lax—the parking lot was free, and so they did not bother to hire security to cover it. There would be no assistance from the fair organizers unless there was evidence that their killer was inside the fair itself, past the fence and ticket gate.

The trooper assigned to pair up with Zoe, a six-foot-four-inch-tall man who had introduced himself as Max but insisted on calling her "ma'am," surveyed their area. "Ready to walk?" he asked her.

Zoe nodded tersely and fell into step beside him. She felt smaller with him at her side, deliberately close together so that they seemed like a couple. Just a couple, walking down the rows back to their own car, or to meet friends, or any number of unsuspicious activities.

But if Max was intimidating, he had nothing on the giant sculptures in the fair. They loomed even from here, where on the flat ground they towered into the distance, rising many feet above the fence. Dusty and sun-cracked in places, they were painted with garish colors, reds and oranges and greens. Camouflage for giant beasts that had nowhere to hide.

At their feet, the stalls were thronging with people. A large part of the crowd was made up of children, excitedly gawping up at the statues and wielding their own dinosaur toys which now paled in comparison. Zoe estimated them in groups of tens and twenties, adding up beyond five hundred visitors—and those were the ones that she could see from this point.

The parking lot, which had seemed overly large on the map, was evidently used to its full capacity at these special events. There were spaces left, but not very many. Zoe saw only twenty percent left at a sweep.

Zoe watched everything around them on either side, numbers and calculations appearing before her eyes everywhere she looked. She saw plates from different states, but none of them on green sedans. There were so many cars in the lot, it was beginning to feel like a much bigger task than anticipated.

She was distracted, tense, on edge. Every muscle in her body felt strained, every part of her mind carefully tuned to look for him. He would be here, she was sure of that. The knowledge put the numbers into overdrive, telling her things she did not need to know.

The exhaust pipe on one car, one inch longer than regulations. The tires on the old pickup truck with less than the legal requirement of 1/16th of an inch tread, coming in at 1/20th. The heavy footprints in the loose dirt where a man of at least two hundred pounds had stood for around ten minutes, the cigarette butt loose next to them explaining why.

"That's it," Max said, coming to a halt.

Zoe looked up and realized she had been about to step over the mental line she had drawn, dividing the parking lot into segments. They were done, and with no luck.

Zoe turned and look across the parking lot. The way she had split the teams, they had all moved from opposite sides of the lot across to the middle, and now stood in more or less a uniform line across the four double-parked rows of cars. All of them stood still, none reaching for a radio to inform the others of a big discovery.

He wasn't here yet.

"Move to secondary positions," Zoe ordered over the radio, hidden in the sleeve of her denim jacket so that she could hold it to her mouth discreetly. "Wait for alert from gate team."

Zoe waited and watched, pretending to look back toward the entrance to the attraction, as Shelley and the troopers all moved off. They had predetermined posts to take up—some of them outside the gates, some of them throughout the parking lot.

"I cannot stand and wait," Zoe said, tilting her head up at Max. "We should walk. We can go over our section again, slowly. Work our way around."

With pauses here and there to make it less obvious that they were actively searching the parking lot, Zoe led Max up and down the rows of the cars, alert all the while. The darkness of night was already coming down, the cars arriving with their headlights on now. It was getting harder to make out the details of the cars, and harder to see license plates—harder to do anything at all.

Zoe admitted defeat when they reached the road entrance during their slow move through the rows, and stopped nearby, leaning on the fence to watch vehicles passing by. Every time she saw something that could pass for the vehicle they were looking for, her heart rate skyrocketed, her eyes catching on comparisons. Tire width, vehicle length, probable age of the driver, height, all played into her mind. But each time, the car drove by, or it was driven by a woman with her kids in the backseat, and couldn't possibly be what they were looking for.

Hours passed. It was a strange feeling, to stand and watch almost in silence for so long, while just a short distance away the riotous noise of people having fun could not be ignored. Children screamed and laughed, carnival games played merry bursts of tune to lure people in, and others thronged from or to their cars while talking loudly. Those with younger children began to leave, bowing to the lateness of the hour. Then the older children, and then anyone at all, as the closing time edged closer and closer.

Zoe watched the parking lot begin to empty out, narrowing down their options. The car still hadn't turned up. If it did now, they would spot it easily. Zoe could feel him out there, moving closer. He had to be getting closer.

She checked her watch and saw that it was past eleven. No newcomers should be entering now. But where was he?

The answer had to be somewhere close by. There was no way he would miss this chance. The pattern demanded a death at this spot, and he would do whatever the pattern required. Zoe knew that—could feel it in her bones. Unless he was dead himself, he would not stop.

So, where was he?

A prickling feeling was moving up and down her arms. At the far side of the lot, a car moved out, revealing something behind. "What's that over there?" she asked, angling her head toward it rather than pointing.

Max looked, squinting his eyes to make out what he could in the darkness. "Looks like some of the fencing got knocked down. Someone's driven through and parked on the grass."

Zoe set out at a stride, not waiting for Max to follow her. "Did someone check it out earlier?"

"I-I'm not sure," Max stuttered, rushing to keep up. "They should have, right? If it was in their section?"

"Ask," Zoe said, handing him her radio. "There is someone at the car. Find out, and then follow me with backup."

She should have taken him along with her; that was protocol. But Zoe had never agreed with the simple math that two heads were better than one. She worked better alone, without someone else's flawed assumptions and calculations getting in the way. She worked better not having to see angles and trajectories and wonder whether her partner was in danger. Knowing her own safety was much easier.

The sound of Max's voice asking the other teams if they had stopped at the boundary of the fence faded into the distance behind her as Zoe moved forward carefully and quickly. She kept her head pointed off to one side, as if she were looking for her car, but her eyes were fixed on the vehicle. A sedan, and no mistaking it. But what was the color?

Zoe watched a man lifting up the hood at a seventy-degree angle to peer inside. The angle of his gaze and the tense, straight line of his shoulders told her that he was having car trouble. Or at least pretending to. The mind flashed to Ted Bundy easily. There were all kinds of ways a man could trick someone into getting close enough to slip a garrote around their neck, and being vulnerable—asking for help—was certainly one of them.

Zoe eased off her pace, remembering to keep her own safety in mind. There was no use in rushing in and becoming a victim herself. In her mind's eye, she sketched the area she had calculated as that which their killer would target. Wasn't this car parked beyond those boundaries? She had suspected it more likely to happen within the grounds of the fair itself, not out here. Yet here he was, if it was him.

He was tall and skinny. Just a smidge over five foot eleven, and the right weight, matching the clues she had seen at the crime scenes. Zoe calculated everything, the numbers flashing in front of her eyes as she moved slowly closer. The car was the right age, the right shape and make. The tires would fit the marks left behind, the correct distance between them, the correct width.

And, as she moved close enough to see clearer, she was sure of it: it was green. An older model green sedan, driven by a tall, thin man, with out-of-state plates.

This is it.

Zoe spared a glance behind her for Max, who was still talking over the radio, but moving step by slow step in her direction. No doubt issuing orders for the others to move in. Backup was only minutes away.

She was close enough now. Close enough to see the color of his shirt and know that his hair was a regular two inches long, at least around the back. No closer. Any closer, and he would be within distance to turn and jump, loop it around her neck and pull.

Zoe stopped and unholstered her gun. For a single moment there was nothing but the dwindling noises from the fair behind her, and silence all around, and the man leaning in to fiddle with something in the engine. He was completely unaware that she was there.

It wouldn't stay that way for long.

"Turn around and put your hands in the air," Zoe called out, raising her gun and dropping into the correct stance to aim it. "Slowly."

The man froze, his hand still within the hood of the car somewhere. Did he think she was talking to someone else?

"FBI! Turn around and put your hands in the air!"

This time, the message seemed to go through. He slowly and stiffly moved, raising his hands a little—only a little—and starting to turn. His right hand was clenched around something, something that glinted in the light coming from the fair as he turned, holding it at chest height. Not high enough. Not safe enough. What was that, glinting like metal? That thin object—could it be a garrote looped in his hand?

"Drop what you're holding!" Zoe shouted, her heart pounding a mile a minute in her ears. Her hands were shaking, and she willed herself to find that calm center and hold steady. Now was no time for nerves.

He flinched at her voice but finished turning, the item still clutched in his hands. The way the light fell, the shadow of the hood cut across his face. She couldn't make out his expression, his eyes.

"Drop it!" she yelled again, loud enough that there could be no mistaking it.

The man seemed to consider it for a single second. His hand moved, as if he were about to drop the item onto the floor.

Or to throw it at her, lunge forward, go on the attack. Zoe's finger tightened on the trigger, ready for him to make his move. Everything slowed, stilled, millennia going by in a single breath as she reacted to his sudden change of posture. Muscles bunched, tensed, kicked, and he was springing away from her, not toward.

The split second of relief was tempered with alarm as Zoe recognized that he was running—making his escape.

He could not be allowed to escape.

She squeezed down on the trigger, trusting her aim, hoping she had guessed the trajectory of his body correctly. There was a flash of light and noise from the gun, and a recoil that snapped her hands back briefly even though she was used to it. Zoe trained her sights on him again, just as she practiced every time she needed to brush up at the gun range, bring the weapon back to aim before she could react to anything else.

He was on the ground, crying out, clutching at his leg. Her aim was true.

Behind her, Zoe could hear the clatter of running footsteps as the troopers moved in. She approached her target cautiously, keeping the gun trained on him, ensuring that the angle and trajectory were always correct even as she stepped closer.

"You are under arrest for suspicion of murder," Zoe said, reading him his rights as she waited for Shelley to step past her and snap a pair of handcuffs onto his wrists. He made no more attempt to move or run, though he gasped in pain and tried to keep his hands clutched on the wound.

And as Shelley finished closing the cuffs, Zoe looked to the ground and saw the object he had been holding, that had caught the light and her attention.

It was the oil dipstick from his car.

No.

Zoe whirled around immediately, dropping the angle of her gun to point it at the ground as she stared helplessly in all directions. Her eyes took in the crowds that were quickly amassing, keeping a respectful distance from the source of the gunfire but wanting to see what it was all the same. Curious faces of families and couples, teenage kids with their friends, grandparents. All attention was on their corner of the parking lot.

Their cover was blown. If Zoe had taken down the wrong guy, they would never find the right one now. He would be long gone.

The arrest was made, and it was all they could do here and now. Zoe returned her attention to the suspect as Shelley helped him into the back of a patrol car that had come flying up the road at the sound of the shot. They had him in custody. She just had to pray that she had made the right call—and that this man was not as harmless as he seemed.

CHAPTER EIGHTEEN

He sat in his car, waiting for an opportunity.

The Kansas Giant Dinosaur Fair was busy, busier than he could have hoped for. Some kind of special event bringing plenty of people his way. Just another example of the pattern making everything easy for him, clearing his way.

He had to be cautious, however. Night had fallen, and hours had passed while he sat in the driver's seat, occasionally shifting his back to prevent getting too stiff. When the fair was at its busiest, it was too risky to attempt an attack. He would be seen.

Besides that, the lights from the fair were bright, and even cast some of their glow this way. He would be better off hunting in the shadows, finding someone who would not be seen until passersby were right on top of them.

There was a point at the far end of the parking lot where the fence had been broken down, perhaps rammed by an over-merry visitor who had forgotten their car was in reverse. Through there, people had begun to drive their vehicles over onto the grass, taking advantage of the extra space to squeeze in. It was here that he kept a careful watch. It was far enough into the shadows that it might afford him an opportunity.

Still, it was a long wait. The stream of cars into the parking lot slowed down and then began to reverse, people leaving with their families. He was getting twitchy now. The balance had to be right. If the parking lot emptied out too much, he would be seen—caught. He had to act in such a way that he would not be noticed.

A man got into his car beyond the fence, a green sedan parked just beyond the real boundary. He turned the engine over a couple of times, only managing a rough grating noise that clearly cut through the distant noise of the fair.

The watcher shifted in his seat, angling himself for a better view, as the man got back out of his green sedan and lifted the hood. Here was potential. Distracted as he was, he would never notice the watcher approaching him. Even if he did, there was opportunity for pretense here: playing the good Samaritan, come to help with the car.

His hand lingered on the car door handle, just about to stealthily get out and make his approach, when a woman came into view.

The watcher let his muscles sag immediately. There was no way that he could approach the man at his car, now that someone else was on the scene. With any luck, she would get into her own car and drive away, before the engine came back to life. Then he would be back on track.

Come to think of it, the woman would have been a better choice. She was smaller and slim, while the man at his engine was tall. It would have been easier to slip the garrote around her neck instead. She was slowing down, coming to a stop just a few paces away. This could be interesting. Perhaps there was a way he could lure her deeper into the rows of cars, toward the edge of the parking lot, away from the potential witness of the man?

But wait—what was that in her hand?

"Turn around and put your hands in the air. Slowly."

The watcher froze, his eyes going wide. A gun. It was a gun.

"FBI! Turn around and put your hands in the air!"

No! Law enforcement—here?

The watcher saw with growing panic how she ordered the man to drop what was in his hand once, then twice. His mind was racing. It was only now that he looked closer and realized that the man was driving a similar car—only green, not red, but like his in all other particulars. Could it be that they knew?

Could they be onto him already?

A gunshot rang out, loud and startlingly close, and the man hit the ground, dropping out of the watcher's line of sight. Had she killed him? Shot him right there, on sight?

There was only one thing on the watcher's mind, and it was escape. That could have been him, lying on the ground now, bleeding out. In agony. The pattern would never be completed if he was shot by the FBI.

No, he had to get out of here—he had to get out right now. Other people were coming running, plain clothed but carrying radios and guns as they ran—they had to be police. Maybe a whole FBI taskforce. The idea of that was a slightly prideful one, that they would send so many people after him, but that could wait until later. Right now, he just had to make sure he was gone before they realized they had shot the wrong man.

He switched on his ignition, the engine roaring to life, and shot out of his parking space. He cursed and had to swerve to avoid a woman with a small child, who were both moving toward the source of the shot and gawking, their mouths wide open. This was not the time to get in his way. He would have run them both down if he weren't surrounded by others, all of them holding guns, some even glancing his way as he peeled around them and out of the parking lot.

A cold trickle of sweat made its way down his spine as he glanced in his rearview mirror again and again, watching unmarked cars speed over to the lot with a determination that seemed deliberate. More undercover units. He passed a group of cars on the shoulder of the highway, the drivers standing and talking with one another. A roadblock waiting to happen.

His fingers were clenched so tightly on the steering wheel that it hurt, and he made a conscious effort to relax them. He eased off the accelerator pedal. Now was not the time to be pulled over for speeding.

Besides, he couldn't go too far away. The pattern still needed to be completed. If he left and didn't come back, it would be broken. He couldn't allow that to happen.

He still needed to make tonight's kill.

CHAPTER NINETEEN

Zoe paced up and down the hall, restless and ready to begin. She had been ready for over an hour, waiting for the doctor to tell them that it was time to interrogate their suspect.

"Sit down, Z," Shelley suggested, patting the empty plastic seat beside her. "We might be in for a long night."

Zoe was just about to give in and sit when the door to the private room in which their suspect was being treated opened.

"You can talk to him now," the doctor said, pausing to lift a finger in warning. "But nothing too strenuous. If his heart rate monitor goes off, I'm going to have to ask you to leave."

"Understood," Zoe said, eager to get inside. She had heard it all before. The gunshot was only to his leg—it wasn't like the guy was in too much danger of further damage. The doctor was just covering his bases.

Which meant she had no qualms at all about pulling out all of the stops to get a confession.

"Stick to the plan?" Shelley asked. They had been going over their strategy for the whole time they waited for the doctors to be finished.

Zoe gave her a quick nod and allowed Shelley to enter ahead of her, getting their suspect's attention first.

"Hello, Mr. Bradshaw," Shelley said, warmly as always. "How is your leg? Did they give you enough pain medication?"

"It's got a hole in it, that's how my leg is," Bradshaw snapped, obviously not taking immediately to Shelley's friendly manner. Zoe could not yet see him properly, still waiting on the other side of the half-open door. "This is ridiculous. I haven't done anything wrong."

"Well, hopefully we can get to the bottom of that now, and you'll be able to recuperate in peace," Shelley told him, dragging a chair over to sit beside his bed. "Let's start from the beginning, Mr. Bradshaw. What were you doing at the Kansas Giant Dinosaur Fair?"

"It's a fair. What do you think I was there for?" Bradshaw snapped.

Zoe had heard enough. Shelley's nice approach wasn't making any headway, and they needed another ingredient. The intimidation that the presence of his shooter would provide might just make him a little more cooperative. She pushed the door open and entered, walking to stand at the foot of the bed.

Zoe assessed him as she leaned on the metal tray holding his charts, resting her elbows on the uncomfortable edges and pretending they did not affect her. His height, weight, and other measurements flashed before her eyes as she gave him the once-over. He was five foot eleven, skinny, a little extra sinew on the arms to equip him well for pulling a garrote.

All seemed to fit what they were looking for, but she still had this bad feeling about him. That the way he acted wasn't at all what she had suspected. He had been unsubtle in his waiting, standing obviously, easily seen. She knew how cautious their man was, how he erased all evidence of his movements as long as he was able to. How would this one have been able to erase his footsteps, after abducting someone in plain view? He had parked on the grass, his feet sinking in, the tires of his car leaving deep impressions. It didn't make sense.

His reaction now was one of wide eyes and a drawing up of his body, shrinking physically away from her. "What's she doing here?" he demanded.

"Special Agent Prime is my partner," Shelley said. "She will be here while I question you. Like I said, Mr. Bradshaw, let's get this over with as quickly as possible so that we can all move on, shall we?"

"Move on?" Bradshaw still watched Zoe, even though he turned his head toward Shelley as he addressed her. "How am I supposed to move on? I've got a bullet stuck in my leg."

"No, you have not," Zoe told him, calmly.

"What?"

"The doctor removed it from your leg."

Bradshaw stared at her, not saying a thing. He looked about fit to explode, a mixture of fear and righteous anger building up inside of him, with no safe target to expend it on.

"Mr. Bradshaw," Shelley began again, then hesitated. "May I call you Ivan? You can call me Shelley."

There was a pause before Bradshaw tore his eyes away from Zoe long enough to mutter, "Fine."

"Let's skip ahead a bit, shall we? When you were asked to turn and drop what you were holding, why did you run?" Shelley's tone was soft and calm. She sounded like she was really curious to know the answer. Zoe knew she would have sounded accusatory with a question like that, and wondered briefly how Shelley managed it.

"Someone was pointing a gun at me," Bradshaw said, his eyes darting sharply back to Zoe on the first word. "What was I supposed to do?"

"Was there no other reason for your attempt to escape? Maybe something you thought you might get into trouble for? Look, we're really here for a murderer, Ivan, so if you've done something else then you can just tell us. We'll get out of your hair."

"I haven't done anything. I was just an innocent bystander. This—this *madwoman* shot me with no provocation!"

Zoe fought down a growl in the back of her throat. They were getting nowhere. She trusted Shelley enough by now to know that she would get through to him, eventually. They might spend hours in here, just talking, before she managed it—but Shelley would break through this anger and fear and get him to really talk.

They didn't have hours. Or, at least, Zoe didn't have hours. She had to know, right now. She had to know that she had the right man. Because if she didn't, then a serial killer was still out there, and still operating on a tight schedule.

The image of the dipstick kept flashing back into her mind, lying there on the grass. The man's car really had been in need of some attention, and it had not been a deadly weapon he was holding. That didn't sit right. Their killer wasn't about to let car troubles get in his way. Their killer was meticulous, studied, precise.

Not only that, but there was nothing in the car that told them anything. No trace of a murder weapon of any kind, not even anything that could be used as a blunt instrument. It was littered with empty plastic bottles and food wrappers on the back footwells, and long blond hairs had been found easily on the passenger seat. If there was anything she knew about the killer, it was that he was clean and tidy. Neat. And he would not leave the evidence of a passenger sitting in his vehicle, easily traceable via DNA.

He would have been waiting with the garrote. Zoe knew that. She could feel it in her bones. Why would he play the innocent victim to such an extent that he was not even ready to attack if someone approached? The only answer she could think of was that this was not their man.

Which was problematic, because she had already been called by her superiors and warned that she was going to be in trouble for firing her weapon if it turned out that the man was an innocent victim.

She needed to get to the bottom of this, and fast. Zoe cast around the room, her gaze flying to the left and the right. Privacy curtain, monitoring equipment, drip, shelving with Bradshaw's clothes...

There—a cabinet. She walked over and opened it, ignoring the conversation behind her as Shelley continued to question him.

"Were you at the fair alone, or were you meeting someone there?"

Zoe rifled through the drawers, looking for something that would work. There wasn't much kept in the room—no syringes or bottles of pills, nothing that a patient could use to harm themselves. But there was a box of Band-Aids. Thinking, Zoe opened it up, pouring them out onto the top of the cabinet with her body blocking Bradshaw's view.

"I was meeting my sister. She had her kids with her, so she went home early. I was going to go home too, but the car wouldn't start."

Zoe began tearing the strips of connected Band-Aids into singles, making quick and regular movements, two or three sets at a time. She dropped each single back into the box in a haphazard manner. She didn't want them to be regular or uniform, not for this.

"Ivan, help me out here. I want to understand so we can let you rest. Just talk me through what was going through your mind, okay? You were at your car, checking the oil levels…"

"And next thing I know, there's someone yelling crazy stuff about the FBI."

"Did you think she was yelling at you at that point?"

"No, why would I? I was just minding my own business!"

Zoe walked back to the bed and yanked a wheeled food tray over Bradshaw's lap. He was watching her with a kind of baffled panic.

"What's she doing now?" he demanded, looking back between Shelley and Zoe as Zoe upended the box and allowed the Band-Aids to tumble out. "Is this a threat?"

The Band-Aids sailed down, scattering across the tray, some of them slipping over to land on the covers of the bed. There was no particular pattern or shape to them, but Zoe knew their guy. She knew he would see a pattern there. She stared down at it herself, starting to organize lines and vertices, checking for the links.

It took her thirteen seconds, but she saw it. Because of the way the box had tipped and the even distribution of the Band-Aids down onto the surface, it had created a more or less distinct sixteen-sided shape. Not an even one, but a shape all the same. The killer would see it—would know it for a sign in his deluded mind.

"What is she doing?" Bradshaw asked again, his voice hissing with fear and confusion, addressed only to Shelley. "I want someone in here with me. This isn't safe."

Zoe watched his face closely. "Do you not see it?"

"See what?" Bradshaw looked down at the Band-Aids again, before raising his head. "See what?"

It was tricky, but there was always the chance that he was faking it. Pretending not to see the pattern. Zoe knew she had to up the stakes, and show him that she knew what he was doing.

He wouldn't be able to prevent his reaction if she drew the one pattern that meant more to him than any other.

She lifted her index finger and slowly, carefully, drew as near an approximation of a Fibonacci spiral as she could in the shifting mass of Band-Aids, clearing out a route like a path through a maze.

But when she looked up, with her task complete, Bradshaw was watching her with even more confusion than before.

"I want a lawyer or something," he said. "You can't do this. This is intimidation, this freaky stuff. She shouldn't be anywhere near me."

"Shelley?" Zoe cut across him, looking over at her partner.

Shelley shook her head. "I was watching his face the whole time, Z. He doesn't recognize the shape. I don't think he has any clue what's going on here."

Zoe slammed her hand down onto the tray, pushing the Band-Aids over onto the floor as she shoved the tray back away from the bed. Another dead end. Another waste of time.

She strode out into the corridor, not waiting for Shelley to follow her, and marched until she found a vending machine. Punching the buttons with more force than was necessary, she waited for the machine to pour out a weak cup of burnt coffee and threw it into her mouth without waiting to check whether it was cool enough.

"Z?"

Zoe turned to see Shelley approaching her cautiously, her steps light and careful. Zoe counted them. One, two, three, four, five. Counted anything, to try to get her heart rate back under control and stop the boiling in her blood at making yet another mistake.

"I told him that we'll send the state troopers to talk to him later. Debrief, get some particulars, see if he really does have anything to hide or not."

"I do not care about Bradshaw," Zoe bit out. "He is not the man we were looking for."

"I know." Shelley sighed, placing a hand lightly on Zoe's upper arm. "Don't blame yourself. We all made the same mistake. We thought it was him."

"It was my idea." Zoe shook her head bitterly. "I was the one who suggested that we go after him. I took the shot."

"Do you ..." Shelley paused, biting her lip. "Do you think we got the wrong place?"

"No." Zoe felt the conviction still strong in her chest, in her forehead. The pattern did not lie. "Right place, wrong man. I do not know how, but he slipped away from us. Now he knows that we are after him, we may not get the chance again."

"Ma'am?"

It was Max, hesitating a good few feet away. He had, perhaps, seen Zoe's violent attack on the coffee machine, and was unwilling to move closer. "We've just had word from the station. The story about his sister checks out. She had gone home with her children just a short while before we approached him. It sounds like he was just there for a day out with his family."

Zoe did not trust her own voice to answer him. It was a relief when Shelley did it for her, simply thanking Max and dismissing him.

"We missed it," Zoe said, as soon as he was out of earshot. She crumpled the paper coffee cup in her hand, a few last drops of the brown liquid dropping to the floor. "We had the best chance to catch him, and we missed it. He will kill again, if he has not already."

Shelley said nothing, but moved closer and rested that light touch on Zoe's arm again. Though it was hardly anything, almost not even there, somehow it was reassuring. A mother's touch, Zoe thought. Something so alien to her that she had not ever understood it.

The moment was broken by the sound of buzzing at her hip, her cell phone vibrating with a call.

Zoe checked the caller ID, cursed inwardly, and then answered. "Special Agent Prime speaking."

"I've received a report that you have shot a suspect while taking him into custody." It was not her direct boss, but the man above him. A serious kind of phone call.

Zoe sighed. "Yes, sir."

"And you've since ascertained that this man was innocent, is that correct?"

There was no point in denying it, or attempting to provide reasoning. "Yes, sir."

"Why do I not have your report on my desk? Why am I hearing this from someone else?"

"We have just left the suspect after interrogation, sir. I am heading back to begin my report now."

"This is not an acceptable mistake, Special Agent Prime. The reputation of the Bureau is on the line. In the current political climate, we cannot have agents going around shooting whoever they want to."

"I apologize, sir," Zoe said, taking a breath to form an explanation—but it was wasted.

"One more misstep on this case and you're done, Prime. That's two wrong arrests, one of them with the incorrect use of a firearm. One more and I'm pulling you out of there. Your partner too."

Zoe's eyes darted toward Shelley. "Special Agent Rose had nothing—"

"I'm sure she didn't, but you work as a team, and I expect you to get it right. The rookie will get off lightly. I'm holding you responsible as senior agent, Prime. If this all goes to hell, it's your job. Do you understand me?"

Zoe wet her lips. There was no other acceptable response. "Yes, sir."

The line disconnected, going flat in her ear, and Zoe dropped the cell back into her pocket.

"Not good?" Shelley winced sympathetically.

"We should just get back to our investigation room. We have only a day before he will strike again—the real killer." Zoe rubbed her forehead in an attempt to clear the heavy headache that was forming there, and set off through the winding corridors of the hospital for the exit.

As they passed the state police moving in the opposite direction to take up questioning of Ivan Bradshaw, Zoe could not fail to notice their scowls. They were clearly unhappy with the direction that the night had taken, and their frustration appeared to be directed solidly at the two agents.

"We just made a mistake," Shelley said, charitably including herself in the blame as she strode along to keep up with Zoe. "We will get him. We still know his pattern. We just missed something this time. Next time, we won't."

Zoe wished she could share Shelley's conviction. The truth was, she had messed up, and she wasn't sure how. And if she made another mistake, it wasn't just her job that was on the line—but an innocent stranger's life.

She picked up her cell again, making one last call to the state troopers. Something had been clicking away in her mind, and now it made itself known. An urgency that came with the realization that they did not have their man after all.

"Hello? I need you to send a patrol back to the fair right away. The man we arrested is not the killer. There is a chance he came late, and we missed him."

"A chance?" The chief sounded skeptical, even through the phone.

"This is an urgent order," Zoe told him, wishing he would just do as she said. "Lives are on the line. Get a patrol back there *now.*"

CHAPTER TWENTY

He drove without really looking, watching his rearview mirror for flashing lights and keeping the window wound down to listen for sirens. The cold air pouring in through the window like waves was the only thing keeping his head grounded in the present moment. The reality of it was a slap in the face, constantly bringing him back to himself enough to stop him from crashing the car.

Without it, he might have been lost. Just as lost as he felt the pattern was, now that he had no chance to complete it.

What was he going to do?

He had failed—he was going to fail. The night was not over, but the cops had known where to find him. They knew where he was going to strike next. It was all over. How was he going to complete the pattern now?

Putting on his turn signal, he pulled over on the side of the road, resting for a moment with his forehead on the steering wheel. Could it really be all over now, so late in the game, so close to finishing it all?

He sat up straighter, realizing something. They had made an arrest, hadn't they? He had seen the FBI woman point her gun and shoot, and the troopers swarming in to arrest that other man and take him away. In his rearview mirror as he pulled out, he had seen them manhandling him, their mouths open in shouts.

If they had made an arrest, maybe they thought they had him. That the suspect for all of the murderers was in custody, and everyone was safe.

And if they thought that everyone was safe, then they would not bother to guard the fair any longer.

With this new thought running in his mind, he started the car again and pulled it in a U-turn back toward the fair. Maybe there was still a chance. In spite of everything, maybe he could still turn this night around.

If he could make it work, then he owed it to the pattern to see it through.

Despite the excitement growing in his blood, fizzing through his veins at a renewed sense of hope, he kept the car steady and smooth. He respected the speed limit, staying just under it all the way, even though there was no longer any sign of law enforcement on the road. He would stay calm, play it cool. Approach them with caution, not rush in without thought.

When he reached the area where the cars had waited in a group as he left the fair—the group that he assumed had been made up of police officers in unmarked cars—there was no one in sight. He slowed down, pulling in on the grass next to the road and switching off his engine. If he was caught here, if someone came to question him, he could just say that he was feeling unwell. That he had pulled over to catch his breath and settle his stomach.

But no one approached, and as the minutes ticked by, he began to feel more confident that no one was watching at all.

He got out of the car, staying close to it in the shadows, even bending over and placing his hands on his knees as another vehicle flashed by in a gleam of headlights on the road. Playing the part. And when still no one came to challenge him, he made up his mind.

It was not too far from the fair, here. He could easily walk to the parking lot and slip through it on foot, right up to the gates. It was closed, past time to allow new visitors, but he could sneak over the fence and see what he could see. Maybe there was still a way to make this work.

He stuck close to the trees, hiding himself in the shadows, glad of his decision to dress in dark colors. This way, he could avoid being seen for as long as possible. If there was anyone still waiting in the parking lot, he could slip away, back to his car and away from detection.

The parking lot was empty. He saw that as soon as he reached the edge of the trees, the broken-down fence he had been watching earlier. It seemed much larger now, without all of the cars to fill it. There was no one in sight, and even the lights of the fair had been turned off. Past the entrance, he saw the tall looming shapes of the dinosaur statues, like sentinels over the empty fair.

No one was here. It was closed, and everyone was gone.

He had missed his chance, after all.

He lingered, wanting to kick something or tear his hair out, fighting back an angry scream of frustration. What was he supposed to do now? There was no one here—no one to complete the pattern. He was never going to make it!

How could he have been so stupid? He should have covered his tracks better—made it less obvious that the pattern was in place. Maybe he should have moved more of the bodies right from the start, since it was the location of the kill that mattered! Why had it taken him so long to realize that? And why had he waited—sat in his car without making a move—instead of just going into the fair to make his attack earlier?

All hope was lost. He contemplated going into the fair and checking, just checking. Even so, a heavy weight had dropped into his stomach, and he did not know if he would even be able to move.

A light flashed out before him, illuminating the parking lot in a wide sweep, and he turned in fear. This night was getting worse by the minute. As the dazzle of the headlights faded from his eyes, he made out the insignia of the state police painted on the side of the car.

"Can I help you, sir?" the cop asked, leaning out the window. His voice had an accusatory tone. It was not really a question of help. The man understood that. It was a suspicion.

He had to think fast—tell him something that would take away the suspicion. Make him a normal person in the eyes of the cop. "I was here earlier, and I think I must have dropped my wallet," he

said quickly, shoving his hands into his pockets in an approximation of glumness. "Thought I would come and check, but looks like
they're closed up for the night."

He waited then, tense. The cop was still inside his car—not an
easy target. Maybe if he would get out, that would be a chance. He
could loop the wire around his neck, catch him, make him tonight's
piece of the pattern. But he had wanted to avoid cops right from the
beginning, avoid anyone that would make too much of a buzz. Cops
wanted cop killers more than any other kind.

The other thing was that the cop might try to arrest him, and
then he would have to do something. Pull the garrote out of his
pocket and stop him before he got the cuffs on or radioed it in. The
man couldn't make out the cop's eyes in the darkness, couldn't read
his facial expression. He had no idea what he would do next. He
couldn't even see how tall the cop was—what if he was too tall, too
strong? He had targeted women for the most part, and for a reason.
That first guy by the farm had almost overpowered him, almost gotten away. He couldn't be sure it wouldn't happen again.

"Well," the cop drawled, making it take longer than it needed
to, setting all of the man's nerves on edge. "You'd best come back
in the morning, son. We're patrolling this area because of an arrest
made here earlier. You can ask the staff tomorrow whether someone turned it in."

The man scratched the back of his head, letting his shoulders
slump. "Yes, sir," he said, dropping into a lower tone, a disappointed
sound. "Guess I'd better just hope for a good Samaritan tomorrow,
then."

The cop rolled up his window and started to peel out, and the
man waited for the car to move before going as if to follow it. He
walked toward the entrance to the parking lot, where it led out onto
the road, as if he was about to walk out and back to his car.

And stopped as soon as the patrol car was out of sight, unwilling
to leave the parking lot just yet. This was where it had to happen.
There was no doubt about that. The pattern was clear. But how was
he going to do that without any target in the area?

He lingered, unsure of what to do or where to go. There was nothing for him here, yet still he felt compelled to stay. All night, if need be, until the sun rose in the morning and it was finally all over.

But he did not have to wait until sunup. In fact, he barely had to wait long at all.

It had been just a matter of minutes since the departure of the state cop when another sound caught his ears. The light laughter and conversation of two voices coming from a distance away, far enough at first that he could hear sounds only and not make out words. They were originating somewhere in the fair, and seemed to be coming closer.

Holding his breath to hear them more clearly, the man crept toward the entrance gates. He stuck close to the shadows at the edge of the parking lot, where the encroaching trees gave him some shade. With a rising pulse, he realized they were approaching closer—close enough that he could soon make out their conversation fully.

Two women, one older than the other. They were talking about their day, about visitors and their behavior and how busy it had been. One of them was jingling a set of keys as they walked. They sounded unhurried, calm, cheerful. Probably pleased at the prospect of another day of work done. He watched them come into view around one of the fence posts, moving toward and through the entrance to the fair.

"Let me just lock up," one of them said, bending down slightly to look at the gate more closely. "God, it's dark out here. I wish they would at least leave the lights on over here so we could see."

"You know what Mark's like," the other laughed. "We're lucky he even pays us to lock up. If he had his way, he'd pay us until the end of the shift and make us work for free."

"Cutting every corner to save a bit of money," the older woman agreed. The other turned on a bright flashlight on her cell phone, pointing it at the gate.

The man held his breath again, examining them in the new light as the older woman finally fit the key into the lock. She was in her late twenties or early thirties, perhaps, her brow furrowed in concentration as she attempted to complete the motion. The other was only a teen, maybe working her first ever part-time job. The perfect way to save up some money for college.

There was opportunity here. The man had never tried for two at once, but they were women, and both of them not expecting anyone else to be around. It was pitch dark in the parking lot without the lights from the fair, and they were on foot, moving toward cars perhaps parked down the road away from the customer area.

Not only that, but the bright glare of the flashlight was in their eyes. As the older woman finished her task at last and shoved the keys into her handbag, the man knew that this was his chance. Once the light was off, they would be functionally blind in this darkness. He would see them, and they would not see him.

This was his chance to keep the pattern going.

He waited until the light went out, and then leaped out from his hiding place to strike.

CHAPTER TWENTY ONE

Zoe punched the pillow, trying to make it somehow comfortable even despite the fact that this felt like a futile effort. There was not much hope for the thin, almost brick-like pillow, if it could even be called that. It was as uncomfortable as anyone could possibly make it, exactly the kind of thing provided in these low-budget motels.

Zoe had not wanted to try to sleep, but Shelley had pointed out that they needed rest for what was likely another long day ahead. Zoe had been in favor of returning to the investigation room and working through the small hours of the night, but Shelley, driving their car, had pulled in outside the motel and insisted.

It was hard to sleep, knowing that you had failed. That you had had a killer in your grasp and still missed him. Just how she had done that, she still struggled to understand. Everything had been right—the car matching the tire tracks, the color the same as the paint under the dead girl's fingernails, all the numbers adding up. The right suspect for the case.

But he had not been the right suspect, and there was no way now that Zoe could hold on to that futile hope.

She had failed, and when she closed her eyes, she saw those dead women staring back at her from the crime scene photos she had spent so long studying. *Not enough*, they seemed to be telling her. *You didn't do enough to stop him.* She had followed up with the state trooper patrols, but no one reported seeing anything.

She rolled over, switching to her other side. The sheets were already tangled around her legs from over an hour of tossing and turning, unable to get comfortable or quiet the noise in her head. She kept going over and over it, the pattern, the numbers, the coordinates on the map. No matter how she looked at it, she felt right. Like there had been no possible way that she had made a mistake on any of it.

And yet the suspect had been the wrong man, all the same, and the real killer had gotten away. Maybe to kill someone else. Most likely, she had to admit to herself. You didn't get this far and then stop because the cops were too close.

Zoe forced her eyes shut again, trying to find something Zen deep inside her that would allow her to relax and drift off. It was not easy. The faces of dead girls swam in her vision, taunting her with her failure. She had failed them. She had failed someone else, someone whose face would join them before long.

She couldn't think about this. She rolled again and tried to crush herself into sleep, squeezing her eyes so tightly shut that her whole face wrinkled inward.

Sometime later, she must have slept. She must have, because her mother wasn't here in Kansas, and therefore there was no way that she could have been standing over Zoe's bed.

"Mom?" Zoe whispered, her voice coming out small and high, the voice of a child.

"Why didn't you pray for forgiveness?" her mother asked, harsh and stinging. "I told you, devil child. You have to beg God to change you."

"I did pray, Mom," Zoe protested. She had. Every night, her knees raw with kneeling on the wooden floorboards by her bed, asking God to change her.

"Then what is this?"

Zoe felt the weight of something thrown down on the covers beside her and flinched. She knew what it was already. It was evidence—signs that she had still been using her power, still seeing the numbers. She should never have written anything down. She had just wanted to remember the calculations, use them to build something of her own maybe. Jenny was the only one in her class who could afford a toy robot, but Zoe had seen all the pieces inside and known how it worked. If she could just get the pieces together—

"You are a wicked child," Zoe's mother said, her breath hot on Zoe's face. "Zoe, you get out of that bed right now and you pray with me. We're going to pray all night long, do you hear me? We'll pray for you not to shame and disgrace us again. Get down here on your knees."

Zoe struggled out of the bed, feeling the hard wood on her tender skin with a whimper, and clasped her hands together.

And it was almost an unnoticeable change into another day when she began to pack her things, getting them all into two single cardboard boxes, everything she had in the world.

"You can't just walk out like this," her mother hissed, flinging words like vipers from the doorway. "We are your *family*, Zoe. Who ever heard of a child doing this to her poor mother?"

"You are not my mother anymore," Zoe said, taking a dress down from a hanger in her wardrobe. "At least, not legally. I can do what I want."

"I bought that dress," her mother said, stepping forward and snatching it out of her hands. "That is mine. You can't have it, devil!"

"There is no devil," Zoe said, tired of this conversation, tired of the same thing over and over again. "There is just me."

"You are the demon." Her mother pointed into her face, stepping forward, broaching her personal space. "You are the devil, you are the evil thing. There never was a child of mine. You were birthed from me a demon. And demon, you will steal from me no more!"

Zoe's mother swiped the box from her hands, sending it crashing to the floor. Clothes and books spilled out, the small number of items Zoe had gathered herself over the years and actually liked. Small, bright pieces of candy scattered in a Fibonacci spiral around everything. Photographs of dead girls spilled out from the pages of books. She itched to reach and pick them up, to turn them over and see what might be written on the back, but they were part of her mother's household now. And this was no longer Zoe's home.

She stared at them for a moment, knowing her mother was going to have to win at least a part of this fight. Legally emancipated or not, Zoe was not going to resort to physical violence. So long as she was away from here, that was enough.

"Okay," she said, and turned and walked out, and that was all.

And she woke sweating, feeling the weight of her mother's hand across the back of her head, reeling for a moment before she realized she was still in a motel in Kansas.

The buzz of a text alert lifted Zoe out of her fitful nap for a second time, forcing her eyes open. Her face was pointing toward the digital clock, and she read the display with a sense of dull inevitability. Of course, she had not made it all the way through to the morning. It was only a little after five a.m., just a short few hours since she had put her head on this rock-hard pillow.

Zoe reached out and lifted her cell phone. She was not properly sleeping anyway, not really, and on a case like this an agent didn't ignore a message. Whatever it was could be crucial, timely. The kind of information you needed to know right away.

She read the message, and felt her heart sinking even lower than she had thought it was possible for it to go.

"No," she said, out loud. "No, no, *no!*"

Shelley stirred on the other bed, her eyes flickering open. "What is it?" she asked, the drowsiness of sleep disappearing as she kicked herself into awareness.

"State troopers," Zoe said, holding back a lump of something in her throat that threatened to overwhelm her. "Two of the fair's employees have been reported missing by their families. They woke up this morning and realized that they never made it home last night. They're putting out an APB for their description and launching a manhunt. Looks like all hands on deck."

"He took them, didn't he?" Shelley asked. She sat up in the bed, her blonde hair falling messily down over her shoulders, mussed with sleep. "Our killer."

Zoe did not have to tell her yes. They both knew.

They had failed to stop him, and now two more women would pay with their lives.

CHAPTER TWENTY TWO

Zoe leaned forward in her seat, wishing the car would move faster. She could see that Shelley already had her foot on the gas as far as it would go, but that did not seem to be fast enough. She held tight to her seatbelt, trying to ignore the motion sickness fighting its way up her gullet in favor of focusing on the task ahead.

Zoe shifted around to look into the back seat. The tall state trooper Max, the sheriff, and one of his deputies were along for the ride. Zoe and Shelley had raced from their motel to their base of operations, and from there straight out to the scene with barely a pause.

Dawn was only just breaking, and they were close by the Kansas Giant Dinosaur Fair, only a few minutes away along the highway. "Anything yet?"

The sheriff shook his head, glancing down at his phone. "Looks like we'll be the first there."

Their quick actions in waking and getting in the car had put them first on the scene. More officers had gone by the residences of the two women to take statements. Two families who had woken in the morning to find beds not slept in, loved ones not come home.

Out of the whole staff, only the two women were still missing. All of the others had left much earlier and were accounted for at home. That much had been ascertained by a simple phone-around.

There was a tension inside the car, each of them knowing that they were not likely to find the women alive. Either one or both of them would have to have been the killer's latest victims. All that remained was to find out which of them it was, and whether he had been fully successful in his crime.

Shelley flipped on the turn signal, trying to turn across the traffic to get to the parking lot. She cursed as she watched her mirrors and the oncoming lane, waiting for a break in busy morning transit of large trucks taking loads across the state. It was only a few seconds' delay before she could get through, but all of them felt it. Every single second counted in a case like this.

Zoe forced the car door open and jumped out before Shelley had even put it into park, her eyes already making out a smudge on the edge of the lot that looked like nothing more than a pile of rags on the ground. Zoe had been to enough crime scenes to know that it was not a pile of rags. It was clothing, and the clothing was on a woman.

From the road, the slight ten-degree slope of the lot hid the body perfectly. Closer up, it was impossible to miss. Zoe spread her arms out behind her as a warning to the others not to approach, and began to carefully and slowly examine the area.

As expected, there were no footprints. The ground was hard, except for the edge of the lot where grass was encroaching back across the surface, but the killer had not made the mistake of stepping in the mud. As Zoe crouched and then shuffled forward, examining everything carefully and tilting her head to get a different angle, she saw no sign that might provide evidence of the sequence of events. The sun was broaching the other side of the highway, rising above the flat land that stretched out a distance away from the trees. Golden light filtered down and over the body, picking out the glints of copper in the dead woman's brown hair.

Golden light for the golden ratio, Zoe thought, inching her way closer as she assessed the victim's measurements. There was blood pooled around the body, though in a tighter and neater circumference than they had seen at the last crime scene. Even so, Zoe calculated that it was as many pints as a body could spare, allowing for the soak into the soil. The woman had fallen here, without much of a fight. She had bled out without moving, perhaps already unconscious from the blood loss or the shock before her heart ran out of blood to pump. Zoe could see a deeper wound to the neck, longer by an inch and a half, though the angle of attack was consistent with the other bodies. The height target of five foot eleven for their killer remained intact.

There was no disturbance to the blood, everything preserved neatly. He would have liked that, Zoe thought. He would have been pleased. But for her, it meant there were no signs or clues indicating what might have happened to the other one.

"It's the older woman," Max said, thumbing his phone screen just behind Zoe. She turned to look at him. "Employee file photos just came through. The teenager is blonde."

Zoe rose off her haunches, addressing Max and the two from the sheriff's station. "Spread out," she said. "Check the trees here, and through the fair. We need to know that she is not still here."

They nodded and moved out, meeting Zoe's curtness with their own silence. Zoe knew she was not going to stand out today, with her short manner that was often described as anti-social or aloof. There was a need to get a job done. Someone's life might still hang in the balance.

Shelley squatted next to her, pointing at the body. "What can you see, Z?"

With the others out of earshot, Zoe crouched again, reading the numbers from the scene before her like they were printed on a page. It was strangely refreshing to be able to share what she could see, instead of keeping it inside. "The victim is five foot six, which maintains our profile for the killer. She is also around one hundred and twenty-five pounds, so not too heavy or strong to cause problems for him. He slipped the garrote around her neck from behind, standing over there, and pulled so hard that she dropped almost immediately. The wound on her neck is an inch and a half longer on each side than with previous victims, indicating a greater force causing a deeper cut. He wanted to be sure this time, after the failure with Rubie."

Zoe got up, circling around to get a better view. "She fell here and did not move after that. You can see this from the blood pool— an almost perfect circle, meaning equal distribution. I would guess that the slight variance on the left side is down to the uneven surface of the lot. It would have taken her around fifteen or sixteen seconds to shed this much blood, which leads me to believe she was either unconscious or in too much shock to move after the attack."

"The teenager?" Shelley asked.

Zoe shook her head, frowning. "Nothing here that I can read. But there was a reason he wanted to get this kill over and done with, why he would have exerted so much force as to cut her neck open this fast. I think they were together. He needed to finish one and go for the other as soon as possible."

Shelley nodded, moving the pendant of her necklace up between her lips and speaking around it. "He took her."

It was not a question. With the facts that Zoe could see, there was no disputing it. Even if the two women had entered the parking lot separately, there was evidence that the killer wanted to move on fast, and the girl was no longer here.

"He came back around after we left last night. This body is less than five hours old. He must be desperate. Maybe he did not want to take a risk on not finding a victim tonight. If he takes a hostage with him, he can be sure that he will be able to carry it out."

Shelley shuddered, getting back up to her feet. "She must be terrified. If she saw her coworker getting murdered..."

Zoe inclined her head in agreement, though she did not see what bearing it had on the investigation. It would not help them to find her and save her life. "Look at the woman's arm. There is a slight indentation above the left elbow. Do you see it? She habitually carried something there, likely a handbag. The muscle is also marginally thicker on this side. No bag left here, however."

"He took it with him to delay the identification process, probably," Shelley said.

"Buying himself time to get further away. Yes, he definitely took her." Zoe nodded, turning and looking into the distance for their local help. All three men had their backs to them, searching. The sheriff was almost completely out of sight in the trees.

"Should we call them back?"

"No, the search has to be done. We have to be thorough. Can you hear something?"

They both turned and looked through the woods again, to see the sheriff raising a radio to his face and speaking into it. Afterward, the crackle came again, the same sound that had filtered to them through the trees. Before another moment had passed, he was moving toward them, taking a determined stride between the tall, smooth trunks.

"Got a hit," he shouted to them, not waiting until he was within hearing distance to pass the message on. "Trooper on patrol last night saw a man come in the parking lot on foot."

"Why did he not stop him?" Zoe asked, bristling immediately. Had this killer once again slipped out from right underneath their noses? Twice in one night?

"Hold on," the sheriff said, coming to a stop close by to them and slightly out of breath. "Trooper, repeat again what you just told me."

"Yes, sir," it came back over the crackle and hiss of the radio. "I saw a gentleman walking through the parking lot after midnight. I asked him what he was doing and he said he'd lost his wallet. I told him to come back in the morning and he began to walk back to his car, which was parked a short distance away."

"Description of the vehicle?"

"A Ford Taurus."

"Color?" Zoe asked.

There was a pause. "Uhh... It was parked on the side of the road, away from any lights. I'm not sure."

"Green?"

"Yeah, could be."

"What about the suspect?" Shelley interrupted.

"Slightly above medium height, maybe five foot ten or eleven, skinny guy. Dark hair, cut pretty close. I would put him mid-twenties."

"Anything else?" the sheriff asked into the radio. "Anything that might identify him?"

"Not that I can think of, sir. I checked my dash cam. There's a glimpse of him, but only his body. He was wearing a gray sweater and dark pants. That's it."

The sheriff sighed and thanked the man, rubbing his tired eyes. "I'll put out an APB."

"It will not work," Zoe said, chewing her lip and looking out toward the horizon. "He is too smart to get caught now. We would have gotten him last night. He knows we are onto him now. It will be that much harder."

The sheriff gave her a hard look. "No offense, Agent, but I've got to protect the citizens of this county. I can't keep running after your theories and missing him every time. You pulling the wrong man last night let this woman die."

He had gone too far. That much was clear. A sheriff didn't speak to a member of the FBI like that, no matter who had superiority. But by the time Zoe could get past the fact that he wasn't wrong, he had turned his back on her to issue orders into the radio, getting his men moving.

Shelley reached over and placed a momentary hand on Zoe's arm, as was becoming her habit. Zoe nodded sharply in response, listening in to the sheriff as he set up a dragnet.

"There's always a chance, I suppose," Shelley said, trying to find some comfort. "We should cover all angles."

"We are still missing something," Zoe said, knowing it with certainty now. "There was no green Ford Taurus in the parking lot at the fair. We would have seen it."

Behind Zoe's words was another nagging certainty. The killer struck every night—and only once every night. There was every likelihood that the teenage girl was still alive.

An alert buzzed on her cell phone, and she opened it to see the photograph of the missing teen, circulated to her number as well as any law enforcement in the area. A fact list named her as Aisha Sparks, seventeen years old. One younger brother. She was a dancer and loved children, wanted to go to college to become a social worker. A good kid.

Zoe stared down at Aisha's sweet smile, in a photograph clearly taken at school for a yearbook, and knew that she had to save her. So many had died already. So many who should have been saved.

If she couldn't save Aisha, Zoe knew, it would all be on her. All her fault. If she was going to redeem herself in any way for letting it get this far, letting him claim more lives, then she had to stop him from taking this one.

Chapter Twenty Three

Shelley was tired of looking over the case files in the investigation room, going over all of the old clues that they had already seen before. The latest autopsy was nowhere near being complete, and they were still waiting for final reports from Rubie's body. There was nothing new here, nothing that they had not already seen with their own eyes before.

It wasn't that Shelley didn't see the benefit of going back over the information—there were many ways that data could take on a new face when you had more clues to go on, when you had seen more victims. Insignificant details could suddenly become the key to unraveling a whole case.

What she objected to, however, was the fact that it was she who had to do it. They were only on their second case together, but already she could see how gifted Zoe was. Shelley was never going to be able to compete with that. She would be better off doing the legwork, physical stuff that didn't require looking at the complex clues. Talking to people. That was what she was good at.

It wasn't that she could really, fully understand what Zoe did. It might as well have been witchcraft, for all it made sense to her. But Shelley was beginning to grasp that just because she didn't understand something, didn't mean it was wrong. She would take anything that she could get to help save lives.

And there was something about Zoe, something that triggered her own mothering instinct, even though Zoe was older than her. Something a little broken, vulnerable. Shelley had known that Zoe had gone through a lot of partners before her. Been warned about

167

it. Now she could see why, and she wasn't going to be the latest in a long line to just abandon Zoe because she had something that set her apart from everyone else.

They had left the door to their room open, allowing in the bustle of the rest of the station from the corridor. A short distance away, the sheriff's office had been the site of much activity all day long, as deputies and state troopers passed in and out regularly.

There was the sound of urgent ringing down the hall, and Shelley perked her ears up. The sheriff answered, barked something down the line, and only a few seconds later strode past the door. He was shrugging his coat on over his shoulders as he went.

"Sheriff?" Shelley got to her feet and rushed out into the hall, looking in the direction he had gone. "What is it?"

"Got a hit with the dragnet," the sheriff called over his shoulder. "Green Ford Taurus. I'm heading out there now."

Shelley glanced back into the room at Zoe, who was still poring over the pages and maps in front of her.

On the one hand, she believed in Zoe. The abilities she had demonstrated were undeniable. The way she had explained everything, Shelley knew she was right. But she wasn't helping here, and every lead had to be followed.

Even if the sheriff was acting in direct opposition to what Zoe thought was the right course of action, at least it was something. And Shelley's time would be better spent dismissing it as nothing than sitting here and wasting her time.

"I should go with him," Shelley said, leaning in to whisper the rest. "I can't tell them why you're so sure they won't find him, can I? So I'd better go."

Zoe looked up and met her eyes, and nodded once with an almost serenely blank expression. "I will stay."

It was exactly what she had expected. There was no reason for it to be any different. Shelley flashed her a quick and reassuring grin, then ran full pelt after the sheriff, catching up with him just as he got to his car.

"Coming along?" he grunted. It was clear from his surly manner and the way all courtesy had been dropped that he resented Zoe's orders. He thought they had taken him on a wild goose chase and allowed someone else to die. So be it. Shelley knew how to turn around an opinion, and the only way to do that was to sit and talk with him.

She dropped into the passenger's seat, waiting eagerly for him to set off. Their car flashed along the roads quickly, moving with the kind of speed and surety that could only come from local knowledge.

"What's the report?" Shelley asked.

The sheriff's eyes flicked toward her momentarily before he focused back on the road. "Green Ford Taurus with a single male driver. The trooper said it looks like he might have been living in the back of his car. Fast food cartons, dirty clothes, that sort of thing. It would make sense, for our guy."

Shelley had to give him that. "No motel bookings for us to track him down with. Have they got his ID yet?"

"Tells us nothing. Out of state, no prior record. They tell me his height fits your profile, though."

Shelley nodded. "Then there's a good chance we have him."

"We?" the sheriff snorted. It wasn't quite an outright denial, and he did not follow it up, but it was clear what he meant. He wasn't putting any stock in the FBI's help on this one.

Shelley kept quiet. There were times when you could change someone's mind, and there were times when it was better to wait out their anger and be ready to make your point only when they had calmed down.

They pulled up at a roadblock perhaps twenty minutes into their journey, where several cars blocked all but one lane, forcing traffic to pass through them. They had a green sedan parked up against the far lane, the driver standing and leaning against his car.

Shelley looked at him with a sinking sensation. The man was overweight, obviously so. He might have been the right height, but he was also older than Zoe had suggested. Either her partner was wrong, or this was yet another wild goose chase.

"I'm telling you, check the records," he was saying as they drew closer.

One of the troopers was talking on his phone, glancing at the sheriff somewhat sheepishly as they approached. Shelley knew what that look had to mean. She felt a groan gathering force inside her, threatening to break out audibly.

The trooper came off the phone and addressed the group at large. "Alibi checks out," he said. "The hospital confirmed he was recuperating in the ward for the last two weeks."

Another dead end. Shelley met the sheriff's eyes, raising one of her eyebrows slightly, hoping that he would get her meaning. They were 0 for 2. And the killer was still out there with an abducted young woman.

CHAPTER TWENTY FOUR

With Shelley gone, the investigation room was a lonely place. Zoe was used to working alone—liked it, even—but she needed some kind of reassurance with all of the mistakes that she had been making. Shelley had been able to provide that.

Hours had passed now without her, as Shelley bounced from one part of the dragnet to another, following useless lead after useless lead. It was incredible just how many green Ford Tauruses there were on the roads, but none of them had turned out to be their killer. There was always something—an alibi, the fact that the driver was a petite single mother without the strength to kill taller women, an incorrect flag with the wrong make of car.

It wasn't that she cared about the cold shoulder she was being given by the local cops. The threat to her job was neither here nor there. Either she would solve it, or she wouldn't. She didn't base her investigative decisions on what would save her job—she was trying to save lives.

It was the fact that they were right.

She had failed—entirely. Another woman was dead.

She felt like a small child again, kneeling at her mother's feet and being told to try again, because she must have been praying wrong so far. She had failed to move God to change her, to rid her of her demonic powers. Now she was failing again, unable to figure out just where they were going wrong in chasing this killer down.

It didn't help that she was closer to solving it than she suspected anyone else could have been. No one else had the insight that she did—the ability to think the same way that the killer did.

That just meant that it was more on her shoulders. If she was the only one who could stop him, then she had to stop him. There was no other choice. The alternative was to just stand by and watch them all die, victim after victim, and there was no way she could do that.

This one had a name already. Aisha Sparks, the seventeen-year-old working at the fair in the evenings to earn enough money to get into college. She was still missing, and if it hadn't been already, it was getting more obvious with each passing hour that he had taken her.

Zoe had watched from the sidelines as the state troopers led a press conference, asking for volunteers to search the local woods around the area of the fair. They were deep and thickly grown, and it would take them many hours to even be sure that they had checked everywhere.

But Zoe knew they would not find her there. There was no chance. He had taken her.

So many had died already. Zoe couldn't let Aisha die as well.

The locations between his killings were getting closer together, the spiral getting tighter now at the end. But the problem was that she couldn't be absolutely, mathematically sure about where he would strike next. Sure, it was a Fibonacci spiral, and that was great—but on the map, even plotting everything carefully, there was still a zone where he could attack next which was not so precise. With the fair, it had been easy—the only thing for miles around, and the scale of the fair itself had filled the whole of the box she had marked on the map.

The little town in the next zone had a number of different buildings. How could she be sure which one he would go for? Or which street? How could they manage to cover all of their bases with such a densely populated area?

And what if Aisha was already dead?

That thought made Zoe's stomach churn, but it had to be considered. The locations in his spiral were for attacks, not deaths. What if he killed her some other way, just to plan to cut her throat after the fact when the time came?

No, that didn't feel right. It would have been too much of a symbolic gesture, a throwaway act instead of the real thing. Somehow, the real thing mattered. It had to be the act of spilling blood at the right moment, the right spot. Zoe could see that. The more she tried to get inside his head and think like he did, the better she thought she could figure out the importance he attached to things. The choice of a new day for each kill, the deliberate action of using the garrote. That had to be followed to complete the pattern.

Yet he had broken his previous MO by abducting a girl instead of finding someone on the actual night, so it was all up in the air now. She could trust her gut, but there was nothing behind it. No real evidence or fact she could put her finger on to tell her that Aisha would still be safe.

Zoe couldn't do this alone. It was too much—so much pressure to heap onto one person's shoulders. She would not begrudge it, not if she could save Aisha's life. But she couldn't get there—couldn't finish the job. Especially not with all the local police turning on her, thinking she didn't know what she was doing.

Zoe picked up her cell and dialed a familiar number from her contact list, hoping that the call would connect.

"Hello?"

Zoe almost sighed with relief. Hearing the voice of her mentor, Dr. Francesca Applewhite, already made her feel better, and all she had said was hello. Talking to someone who understood her completely was a salve for all of the stress.

"Dr. Applewhite," Zoe said. "Are you free to talk?"

"Francesca, as I've told you a million times," she laughed. "Yes, I'm free. I'm always free for you, even in the middle of a session. But I don't have any appointments today. It's Saturday."

Zoe glanced at her smartwatch reflexively, surprised to hear the date. Time had been slipping away from her, maybe faster than she had realized. "I am sorry to disturb your weekend."

"You don't have to be sorry with me, Zoe. You know I don't mind. Now, what's bothering you?"

Dr. Applewhite always understood when Zoe needed help. "It is regarding a case I am working on," she started, and quickly told her everything. Or at least, everything that was relevant. With it being an ongoing case, she could not use names or even give away the locations precisely. But it was worth taking the risk of being sanctioned if it meant getting some help from the one person who always knew the right thing to say.

Now Dr. Applewhite was chuckling, and Zoe could not quite understand why. "What is funny?" she asked, seeing nothing amusing at all in the tale of a serial murderer and schizophrenic.

"The pattern," Dr. Applewhite replied. "Our boy here has it all wrong. He might be operating under delusions, but they are bigger than he realizes. He has misunderstood the reality of the Fibonacci spiral."

"I do not understand."

"It's like this. The Fibonacci spiral is a theory, a formula that can be applied to many visual patterns in nature and that are naturally occurring. But the mistake the killer has made is assuming that the spiral should be perfect. In fact, in nature, it is almost always imperfect."

Zoe frowned. "But I thought the point was that it is a specific sequence. Each number the sum of the two previous."

"Yes, but nature is not so neat as mathematics might have you believe. Think about the instances where we can see Fibonacci spirals: a snail's shell may grow slightly tilted. A plant's leaves may experience growth spurts due to exposure to water or light that can throw off the pattern. A hurricane fits within the spiral, but it does not have well-defined and sharp edges. Wind forces clouds to stream back alongside the spiral itself, making a feathered edge which does not always conform exactly to the pattern."

Zoe got the point. "So the pattern should be imperfect. But how does that help? If it is imperfect, we have even less chance of catching him."

"No," Dr. Applewhite said, and Zoe could almost hear her smiling. It was the same look she had always had on her face when making an important point, knowing that she was delivering important knowledge to her student. "The mistake that the killer has made is believing that the pattern *should* be perfect. It will be precise—exceedingly precise."

Zoe turned this over in her head. "He is so obsessed with the pattern that he cannot see the fact that there are variances in nature. His pattern will have to be perfect."

"Just the same way that you, my dear, sometimes find it hard to look past the numbers in order to see the variances of human nature. How you can struggle to understand the subtleties of small talk or emotional responses, because you are watching the calculations in your head."

Zoe bowed her head slightly over the table of maps and papers. Dr. Applewhite was right. Even though she was the only person who had the ability to see things as the killer saw them, that also meant that she was victim to the same mistakes and foibles.

Being the same as a serial killer—that sent a shudder through her again.

"There is beauty in imperfection," Dr. Applewhite continued. "Our flaws are what make us human. That's why I have never judged you for yours. But this perpetrator... he does not see the beauty. He is incapable of looking past the numbers of the spiral itself. He objectifies it, just the same way that a serial killer looks at a victim instead of seeing a wife, mother, sister, friend. The end goal is all that matters to him. Because of this, he has made himself a predictable man."

"You mean that we can be more precise with the calculations. Find out exactly where he intends to commit the final murders, to a much closer degree."

"Yes. Why look at a whole town? He can only see a precise coordinate. You could take it down through decimal places, rather than looking at whole grids on the map."

"I understand," Zoe said, grabbing a pen. "I have the precise coordinates of each of the attacks." She was starting to scribble out calculations, make the numbers smaller.

Dr. Applewhite laughed, a sound of joy and friendship that never failed to warm Zoe's heart. "Hit me with the numbers."

Zoe hadn't thought to ask for help, but it was welcome. There was always a security to be found in your work being checked. Even though she had already completed the calculations, there was no harm in accepting the offer. She flicked through each case file to read out the coordinates to four decimal points, waiting for Dr. Applewhite to run the logarithmic function and determine precisely where the next points would be. There were only two left, and that made their job easier—they had almost all of the clues, and none of the mystery. It took time to input the data—time Zoe desperately wished she had spent earlier in the investigation—but then it was done, and they had what they needed.

"All right," Dr. Applewhite said, after a moment's pause for the calculations. "Take down these numbers."

Zoe checked them against her own and saw that they matched, then used the battered old computer in the corner of the investigation room to input them in a map search. "Got it," she said, focusing in on the square highlighted on the search. "Thirty square meters. Close enough that we can watch it all at once."

"Well done! And will it be an easy target to stake out?"

Zoe studied the map again, checking that she had not made a mistake. "It is a diner," she said. "It looks like the whole space is taken up by the building. I will have to check with the local authority that this map is accurate."

"No—the killer wouldn't have been able to do that," Dr. Applewhite pointed out. "He is going on the same data that you have. A publicly available map. Trust in what you see."

"Then it is only part of the building. The front area, facing the street with the entrance doors, is not even included. The full boundary encompasses only the middle and back part of the diner."

"You know where to find him. I suppose you had better hurry—didn't you say that he always strikes after dark?"

Zoe checked her watch. In the isolated, windowless investigation room, she had not even noticed how far along the day had progressed. It was nearly time for the sun to start going down, and after that it would not take long for him to strike.

They needed to move—and now. She would have to travel along his route, figuring out the roads he would take, where he would be. There was still every chance that Aisha was dead, that he would only arrive to dump her body. Or that she was alive but would not be by the time he reached the diner. Zoe would have to keep her wits about her, and her eyes open.

Leaving the math behind, breaking away from the pattern, felt uncomfortable. Zoe thought it would be the same for the killer, but how could she really know? As much as she understood the numbers with an instinctive resonance, the human mind was something else altogether. That was what truly terrified her and made her heart jump into her throat: the idea that he might deviate now, at this late stage.

"Thank you," Zoe said, breathlessly, into the phone.

"Don't mention it," Dr. Applewhite said. "You can show your gratitude by booking an appointment with that therapist I recommended."

"I will talk to you soon." Zoe signed off with a small smile, unwilling still to commit.

There was not much time to be wasted on pleasantries, after all. Zoe knew where the killer was going to be, and she knew when— and it was soon. She ended the call and dialed Shelley's number instead. They would have to meet there—she could not wait for her partner to get back to their base of operations when someone's life was going to be on the line.

CHAPTER TWENTY FIVE

Zoe sat at the counter, alone. She was nursing a cup of coffee, but barely drinking it. Instead, she occupied herself by looking around, checking every direction on a regular basis.

She could not stand the waiting. She had considered every angle, every option. That he would bring Aisha in alive, then kill her in the middle of a room full of people. No, that didn't make sense. That he would bring her in dead—but how would he expect to leave there alive afterward?

Zoe had spent her time approaching the diner carefully, checking the roads, the parking lot, looking inside every car parked there. Not just Ford Taurus vehicles of any color. She was not going to make that mistake twice. No, she had looked over everything thoroughly, and there was no sign of him.

But there was a little light of hope remaining in her heart. This was the fact that there were two kills remaining, not just one. Two locations. And maybe, just maybe, the killer would keep Aisha for last, to make sure his final point would not be ruined.

That made more sense than trying to kill a girl, or bring one already dead, into a crowded diner. He must have known that this would be his ticket to the inside of a jail cell.

And then again, with a schizophrenic off his medication, how could you know that his mind would work logically?

But Zoe had to take a stab. She was only one person, and she could not be everywhere at once. She had alerted Shelley to move in carefully and cover a wider area with the state troopers, observe the parking lot, keep eyes everywhere they could. They were stretched thin with leads in so many different directions now, and the stakes were high. One little movement in the back of a car could indicate Aisha's struggle. Something easy to miss before her life was over. But the troopers would be out there on the road, in the lot, waiting.

And Zoe was left watching the diner. It seemed unlikely that he would find a victim here, didn't it? But there were private spaces—the kitchen, the bathrooms. Places a little more out of sight. She just had to watch for suspicious behavior somehow. If he came in, she would see him. She would stop him. She swore that to herself.

There were ten booths at the sides of the room, with a wider central area containing several tables that were easy to see in a glance. Then there was also the counter. That allowed twelve places where the killer could possibly be—fourteen, if she counted the bathrooms. She had already checked out the ladies' room on entering, in case he would lurk for a victim there. A trooper she had never seen before had come in, looked around the men's bathroom, and left again with a subtle nod to Zoe earlier. His job done, he had returned to watching cars. There was no killer here—not yet.

Zoe tried to keep her knee from jiggling up and down, to keep the numbers from overwhelming her. She knew the height and weight of every person in the whole place, from the waitresses who swirled around with pots of coffee and order pads to the twenty-seven others sitting in various positions around her. The diner was busy—almost full. He would not have to look hard for a victim, though the challenge would be in taking a life without being seen.

Zoe was determined that she should see him.

She tried not to let it bother her that there was one more sugar dispenser than there were salt, and that there were two more of each than there were tables—spares, taken at some point into circulation and then left to occupy odd spots rather than tidied back away. She tried also to ignore the seventeen burgers, twenty servings of fries, twenty-eight coffee cups (some not yet cleaned away after being abandoned by their previous owners) and four milkshakes on the tables. These things, she did not need to know.

She did not need to know that there were seven empty seats, but only one totally free table. There was no reason for her to know that there were thirteen light fixtures dotted around the room, or three air conditioning vents, or that the waitresses each wore their apron strings at a slightly different length.

What she did need to know was everything possible about the people already in the diner, and she applied herself to this with as much effort as she could. She turned her back to the counter and leaned, surveying the room in a way that she hoped seemed casual. She ordered a second cup of coffee and set it down next to her, as if she were waiting for a friend.

Over half of the occupants of the diner were female, the ratio weighted by the wait staff made exclusively of women. Several were also children. Zoe could dismiss those out of hand. Then there were the overweight men, a familiar sight in an establishment that served mostly sugary or fatty food. Two of them were far too old, of retirement age, lacking the necessary arm strength to do the deeds.

That left five men, one of them being too short to reach the necks of the tallest victims without difficulty, meaning that Zoe could rule him out. Down to four.

Groups sat in obvious structures, patterns dictated by social expectations. Man—woman—child, family unit. Girlfriend opposite boyfriend. Two girls facing two boys, sweethearts sitting together. Predictable and strong. But there were those she could not place—two men and a woman, she on her own while they faced her, no clear lines of family or love. Those were the most enigmatic, the ones that forced wonder the most.

A group of three—a man, woman, and child—got up from their seats and left. That gave her three. But another party was coming in, four young men, not much older than teenagers. That brought her back up to seven, and they were followed by a young couple. Eight, now. Another couple were getting up to leave, freeing up one of the booths, and—had she eliminated that one already? Was it seven or still eight?

Zoe furrowed her brow and concentrated. She had to get this right. It was not certain that the killer would be easily apparent, on the surface. He might be a local—might have planned to end up here, even despite their assumption that he came from out of state. That meant he could be with friends, even family members.

Zoe had felt he would be a loner, but maybe that was just her own bias. She was, so he should be. Maybe he wasn't like her at all, and could maintain relationships and have friends easily in spite of his way of seeing things.

Maybe not.

The dinner rush was starting to cool down, the sun already set outside. Another group got up to leave, having finished their evening meal, taking the kids back home to sleep. That was one of her suspects. She was at seven now, for certain. She surveyed the group of four male friends, trying to take them in, to wonder if one of them was looking around too much or seemed nervous.

The door opened again to allow in a young man on his own. He looked unremarkable: plain but respectable clothing, five foot eleven, slim. He sat a few stools down from Zoe, past an overweight trucker and a woman who had checked her phone eighteen times in the last ten minutes.

The young man ordered a tea, and Zoe watched him from the corner of her eye, as best as she could past those in between them. It was possible. He could be the one. Zoe added him to her mental tally and did another sweep of the room, watching the other tables, eliminating one man for his messy eating habits.

The woman sighed and got up, leaving quickly with her head ducked down. Zoe glanced to the side. She could see the young man a little better now. He, too, seemed to be surveying the room.

Another family group got up and walked out, a single mother with three children in tow. Zoe watched the door, but no one else came in. Where was Shelley? Surely she would arrive soon?

The trucker threw some cash down on the table to pay his bill and got up, letting out a belch as he did so. Zoe looked at him, unable to stop herself. As he moved away, her eyes met those of the young man, who looked similarly disgusted.

For a second, they held one another's gaze. There was a flicker in his eyes, something that she could not quite pinpoint, before he looked away.

Zoe continued to watch him. He was studiously not looking toward her now. There was no doubt about that.

That glimmer. Could it have been … recognition?

Zoe's mind raced. Height, weight, age. All of it added up. The timing of his entrance to the diner, after the sun had completely gone down. The fact that he was alone, while the other single men in the diner looked to be there for a purpose—truckers stopping on a long journey, dates anxiously waiting for their partners, and one man in a rumpled suit who Zoe had pegged as an alcoholic trying to sober up before going home.

This young man—he was there for a reason as well.

He was there to kill.

She knew it in her bones. It was him.

There was only going to be one shot at this. If she messed up, he could get away. Showing her cards as an FBI agent would force the real killer to run, if it wasn't who she thought it was. But she felt sure. It had to be him.

Zoe stood, about to go over and question him, just at the same moment that he also got up from his seat. She hesitated, pretending to adjust her jacket, as he walked over to the back of the diner and entered the bathroom. Thwarted, Zoe sat again, thinking that she would have to wait until he returned.

She grabbed her phone and fired off a quick text to Shelley. A warning, but not yet an order for backup. *Suspect sighted. Gone into bathroom. Waiting to approach for questioning and arrest when he emerges.*

Zoe waited, keeping the bathroom door in her peripheral vision so that she would see it as soon as it opened. Another man went into the bathroom, Zoe's skin prickling as she tried to catch a glimpse of anything beyond the door as it swung shut.

A quick glance around the room at her other suspects, none of whom seemed to be anywhere near as interesting.

The bathroom door opened again, and Zoe looked around, her body tensing—but it was only the other man coming out.

Her blood rushed in her veins. It had been long enough for the second man to go in and come out—why not her suspect?

What was he doing in there? Was he trying to escape?

Had he already climbed out the bathroom window and run out of sight, to where she would have no clue about where to track him down?

There was only one thing to do. Zoe took a sip of her coffee for fortitude and got up from the stool. Checking her gun in its holster with a light tap, she headed resolutely for the bathroom, avoiding eye contact with anyone around her as she deliberately entered the men's door.

Zoe drew her gun as she stepped through, letting it shut behind her. The last thing she needed was a civilian coming in at the worst possible moment. She considered locking the door, but that would only trap herself as well as the killer.

She gave a quick glance around, moving with the gun pointed ahead of her as she had been trained. The urinals were abandoned, the sinks empty. One by one, she moved past the stalls. Each of them were open, doors hanging in such a way that she could see there was no one inside.

The bathroom was empty.

The window was open, a predictable conclusion to the lack of any occupants. Zoe looked up; the aperture was wide enough, she calculated, for a man of his slim bulk to fit through. The shoulders may have been tight. She approached and touched the glass, finding that the pane opened further upward, going flat in such a way that it would have allowed him one more inch. Just enough, leaving a spare centimeter and a half of wiggle room. He would have made it.

Zoe moved closer and stood on her tiptoes, relaxing her posture with the gun as she peered out of the window. There was nothing to be seen outside, no mark that he was nearby, no footsteps on the ground that she could make out. Not even from the impact. He was not a heavy man, but surely he should have made an impact…?

Too late, Zoe realized the truth. He had not leaped out the window at all; that was why there was no evidence of it. She heard the creak of a door behind her and dimly remembered seeing a janitor's closet, and one footstep on the tiled floor, and she knew that she had made a mistake in turning her back on him.

Instinctively, Zoe's arm shot up, holding the gun. She wanted to turn and point it at him, but there was no time.

All she succeeded in doing was catching her arm in the wire that was intended for her neck, her hand and wrist knocking into her own face as he pulled tightly, drawing it into a loop. She managed only to articulate a strangled gasp as she dropped the gun, flinching as it hit the floor with a loud clatter.

It was sheer luck that it did not go off—good or bad—perhaps it might have hit him if it did. But he was pulling resolutely, hard, with the same determination that had dispatched all of his victims so far. Zoe heard herself cry out involuntarily as the fabric of her jacket gave way, the wire cutting through into the flesh of her arm.

She could not go down like this. She could not allow the three-centimeter wound to grow larger, could not allow the wire closer to her neck. The killer had a strong grip, but he was off balance, his usual stance thrown off by the interference of her arm.

She threw the other elbow back, connecting fully with his lower chest, hearing him wheeze as some of the air was knocked out of him. He stumbled back but took the wire with him, making Zoe cry out again as the wire bit deeper into her skin. She could feel hot blood running down her arm already inside her sleeve, pooling inside the material where it bent.

He was standing just an inch or an inch and a half outside of her elbow range now, still pulling hard, the wire so sharp Zoe feared it might go through her arm before she could defend herself. He was bent forward slightly in her peripheral vision as she turned her head, his neck bent at thirty degrees, his hips at sixty. Top-heavy.

Unbalanced. Humans had been designed with finesse, but they had weak points.

Zoe dropped to her knees, going down without any safety net, knowing it would likely hurt. Her kneecaps collided with the tiled floor with a dull thud that echoed through her body, shaking more blood from the wound of her arm, splattering it across the tiles in front of her. A clue for investigators in the future. The killer held on tight, but as the wire dipped under the weight of Zoe's body dropping, he was pulled further off balance, tumbling down with her.

His body struck hers with a heavy weight, shoulder colliding against spine, head glancing off shoulder. They were on the floor and Zoe was free of the wire at least for a moment, falling loose like a halo around her, but her arm was gushing blood and the gun was out of her reach on the other side of the bathroom...

He saw it at the same moment that she realized it, and then they were both lunging for it, fighting to get their hands on it first. Zoe undercut him at a leaner angle and knocked him out of the way, down again, as she struggled to her feet. The wire forgotten behind her, she had not a moment to hesitate as she saw him lunging forward again. She had not succeeded in winding him a second time. He would reach it first.

She had to *do* something. In desperation, Zoe whirled, seeking something that would provide a moment of advantage. Distraction. There! Flinging out her elbow, using the arm that had already been damaged, she struck a mirror and shattered it into pieces.

"Look!" she shouted, her voice underpinned by the tinkling of shattered glass falling down. "The pattern!"

The killer glanced back toward her, startled. She saw his eyes change, widen, in recognition and surprise at the understanding. His gaze darted then toward the floor, as if unable to resist. The glass was settling, some of it fallen into the sink, some in a semi-circle around it on the floor. The empty space within, the curved shape, the spray of errant pieces—it was irresistible to him.

Zoe leaped forward and got her hands on the gun as she slid along the floor. Her shoulder hit the back wall, and she ignored the pain racing through not just that spot but her whole arm as she rolled to raise the gun. She got it up in front of her, waiting for the world to stabilize just long enough to see him lunging for her again, and she pulled the trigger.

Point blank range, almost. Only a millisecond more and he would have been on her. Even if she hadn't known how to aim, she almost certainly would not have hit him.

He slumped to the floor, taken back a few inches by the impact of the bullet, and raised a hand to his chest to examine the hole that had suddenly appeared there.

Zoe panted for breath, adrenaline washing over her in waves. She felt faint, light-headed. Looking at the blood smattered around the disordered bathroom, she thought she knew why. Things were getting fuzzy as the world cleared and settled, the ringing of falling glass in her ears, the mad dash for the gun and for breath, the hot wet slick of her right arm.

The silence might have been a second or an hour; Zoe watched dully as the killer's hand fell back down against his own leg, energy draining from him as quickly as the lifeblood surging from his chest. He had a strange look on his face, unreadable to Zoe. She had shot well. She knew she must have been close to the heart, if not a direct hit.

The bathroom door burst open, simultaneous with a familiar shout of, "FBI! Put your hands in the air and drop your weapon!"

Shelley appeared in the empty frame, stepping forward with her gun trained on the killer as she assessed the scene in a few glances. "Zoe?"

Behind her, Zoe dimly heard other cops shouting orders to civilians, evacuating the diner. Shots fired. That must have caused a panic.

"Where is she?" Zoe asked. She needed to know. Aisha Sparks was not here—he had not brought her to the diner after all. He had been looking for someone new. So where was the girl?

The killer was laughing, Zoe realized, his mouth gaping open and his chest shaking even though barely any noise escaped his lips.

He did not answer her. His mouth was twisted into a rictus grin, his eyes fixed on Zoe's with a spark that said they shared a secret. Something she should have understood.

And in a flash, she did understand.

Zoe knew why he laughed. Why he was happy at the moment of death.

He needed someone to die here. And now, with a last wheeze that emptied his whole body and stilled the manic joy in his eyes, someone did.

"Where is she?" Zoe yelled, throwing herself across to him, grabbing the front of his shirt to shake him. There was no response. There was never going to be a response again. It was over. Zoe slumped back, raising her eyes to the ceiling and letting out a groan of impossible frustration.

"Talk to me, Z!"

Zoe returned her attention to Shelley, nodding briefly. "I am okay," she said, impatiently. She did not want to bother with formalities and niceties, nor was she concerned at all about her own health. Aisha Sparks was still out there, and he had given them no clue at all as to where.

"Bleeding?" Shelley said, pointing as she crouched to get level with Zoe.

Zoe glanced down at her own arm, as if she was surprised to see the saturated red fabric of her jacket. "Oh, yes," she admitted, feeling detached and foggy, her mind's eye still fixed on that laughing grin. "He did get me with the wire."

Shelley swore, barking orders through the doorway at the cops piling into the room after her. "Get me an ambulance, now! I have an agent heavily losing blood!"

Chapter Twenty Six

"I do not need to go to the hospital," Zoe repeated, for the third time.

She sat in the middle of chaos, on the tailgate of an ambulance, as law enforcement buzzed around her. They had already carted away the body of the killer, taken him to a local morgue to be analyzed and prodded into giving up his secrets.

"Are you sure?" Shelley asked, exchanging a glance with the EMT. "I really think it would be better if you went to get stitched up. It's over now. You can go."

"It is not over," Zoe refuted, raising her arm and holding it toward the EMT. "Finish patching me up. We still have to find the teenage girl."

Shelley sighed and folded her arms, but she did not object again as the EMT started to wind a white bandage around the quick job he had done on Zoe's arm.

"This is a temporary solution," he warned, finishing it off. "I do advise you to make your way to the hospital for stitches at the earliest possible opportunity. And no exerting yourself, especially not with this arm. You could end up causing further damage."

"I will go in as soon as we find her," Zoe said, hopping up off the trailer and making her way over to Shelley. She eschewed the jacket that was now altogether ruined with blood, grabbing a windbreaker someone from the state troopers had left for her to cover her similarly bloodied shirt.

She stood next to Shelley, watching the crime scene team swarm the whole diner as well as the killer's car in the parking lot.

The car: a red Ford Taurus, seemingly a repaint of a vehicle that had once been green. At the very rim of the hood, a few chips of paint had flaked loose, revealing the original finish underneath. It was here that another chip was missing, the green gone to show just the metal frame; the chip that had turned up under Rubie's fingernail.

The hive of activity was centered on two things: collecting traces of evidence to back up Zoe's claim of self-defense against the man who was surely their serial killer, and looking for any insight on what he had done with his hostage.

"He finished it."

"What?" Shelley asked, looking around at Zoe with surprise.

"He finished the pattern. That is why he looked so pleased with himself as he died."

It had been playing on her mind since the moment she shot him. She had expected despair, not just at his impending death but also at his failure. For the killer, the pattern had been everything. He would not have been happy to leave it incomplete.

He had been laughing because, to him, the whole thing really was funny. The pattern was complete, and he himself was a part of it. Now, in a flash of inspiration as the fog of pain and shock from her confrontation cleared, she understood what that meant. He would not have been happy to die if he had not finished everything—including the last point on the spiral.

How had she not realized it sooner? Cursing blood loss and the emotional reeling from killing a man, Zoe knew that action was needed—and now.

"He took Aisha Sparks somewhere," Zoe asserted. "He set her up somewhere to die. And I know where."

"The last point of the spiral," Shelley said. She might not have been able to see the patterns like Zoe could, but she wasn't dumb. She understood the concept. "You think he set something up so that she will die tomorrow night."

"He must have known that we were getting closer. We were almost upon him at the fair, and he was seen by the patrolman—he must have known there was a good chance that he would not make it through this night."

"Only one more death needed to complete the pattern. So you think she is already there?"

Zoe nodded. "We have to search it. Gather a team from the state troopers and call the sheriff to send men. I will go to program the GPS."

Shelley hesitated, glancing at Zoe's arm. "I'm driving."

Zoe rolled her eyes. An easy concession to make if it meant that they would get on the road. "Fine."

She waited in the passenger's seat with restless energy. The girl would be there. The maps, which Zoe had photographed with her cell so that they would always be able to check them on the move, indicated a new area for the final point of the spiral. With their new, more precise logarithm, it had been narrowed down significantly. It was a small area: a road, two houses on either side of it—each of them offering only their front rooms, with the back of the houses and their gardens out of the correct zone—and a small portion of a railway line.

It was precise, but it would still need searching. If she needed someone to die, where would she put them? Out of sight, certainly. A basement or an attic. Somewhere that they wouldn't be found, much less suspected.

Shelley swung into the driver's seat, still signaling with her hands to a group of men who were, in turn, dashing to patrol cars. She started up the engine, looking at Zoe.

"What are we looking for, do you think?" Shelley asked, moving the car away from the diner, taking it slow as she dodged people coming to and from official vehicles.

"I know as much as you," Zoe sighed. "No special powers on this one, I am afraid. He needs her to die tomorrow, so we have at least until dawn."

"Not after nightfall?"

Zoe shrugged, feeling a dull throb in her arm as she did so. "We know only that he attacked after dark to avoid raising suspicion.

Maybe it was never about the time of day. Maybe it was. I do not know for sure, and we cannot ask him."

Shelley sped up as they pulled away from the scene, and Zoe grabbed hold of the seatbelt, forcing it away from her neck. She fought down a wave of nausea. Car sickness was even stronger, it seemed, when you had lost enough blood to warrant a hospital visit.

"How are you doing, about that?" Shelley asked. Her eyes flicked between the rearview and side mirrors and the road, checking that the rest of their small team were keeping up.

"About what?"

"Killing a man," Shelley said plainly, then bit her lip. "I've never had to fire my gun yet. You've done it twice in the last two days."

Zoe sighed again, shutting her eyes momentarily. The motion was no less sickening without being able to tell where she was going. "I am fine. For the moment. Later, I am sure that one of the Bureau's appointed psychologists will tell me how fine I am not."

Shelley laughed at that, a kind of strangled, guilty noise. "You shouldn't joke about that."

"Who said it was a joke?"

Shelley smiled, settling back into her seat a little. Zoe saw her hands relax on the wheel, going from a stiff and straight position to a more casual crook in her elbows. "Still a few hours until dawn. We have a good chance."

A good chance, except for the fact that they would be searching in the dark. Zoe knew that the percentage of success went down in such a situation. Vital clues could be missed. Still, she did not want to air such pessimism. "We have to find not just a hiding place, but a method of murder. We have to be careful. No blundering around. He may have set up a trap which will kill her when she is found."

Shelley made a sympathetic noise. "I hope not. Poor doll must be terrified. She's only a teenager."

"She may well be sedated. He has to keep her in the same place, no chance of her escaping. He planned to not be there when she died. Maybe even if he got away tonight. Fleeing the state entirely would have been the best course of action."

Shelley chewed her lip, barely slowing down as she took a corner at high speed. "Hidden, trapped, sedated, and primed to die. But how?"

"That is what we need to figure out. And quickly." Zoe took a deep breath, winding down the passenger side window a little to get some fresh air. "Before his plan works."

The journey was filled with useless speculation. Zoe tried to focus hard on her thoughts to ignore the pounding in her head, the throbbing of her arm, and the sick feeling trying to claw its way up her throat every time Shelley turned the wheel or put her foot down on the accelerator.

The site was not far from the diner, a route that took them only thirty-five minutes to drive. But the timer was still ticking down, as far as Zoe was concerned, and it was ticking down loudly in the back of her head. Sunrise: that was when she felt that all bets might be off. When he might have set it up so that Aisha Sparks would never see another one.

The troopers gathered for their instructions, Zoe's eyes working over all of them. Their heights were mixed, their weights all within a healthy range. The kind of men and women who would be able to search for hours, with good physical fitness and the ability to look both high and low. There was every possibility that this was going to be a long night. They needed the best the state had to offer.

Working quickly, they marked out the boundaries of the search area on foot. Zoe disseminated the marked-out map zone to their cells, and they set up a roadblock at each end of their box with a trooper stationed there to man it. That left them with ten people in total, including Zoe and Shelley. Three each to wake the residents of the house and carefully peel through all of their rooms. Two on either side of the road, moving through the grass and empty land, combing for any sign.

For safety's sake, they expanded their area to include the back rooms and gardens of the house, as well as the houses directly on their northern side should the search come up empty.

Zoe moved with Shelley to the southern zone on the east side of the road, carrying torches and moving close together as they walked in a grid pattern. Up, then across, then down, then across and up. Thorough and slow. They looked for disturbed ground, items that might have been discarded by either the killer or Aisha, any sign at all that an intruder had been here.

Zoe saw formations of weeds indicating the spread of seed in the wind, and she noted a worn-down path indicative of lazy feet shortcutting through the grass on their way to the road. She saw a deflated ball that told stories of local children playing in the area, but there was no dug-up and replaced soil. No dropped trinkets or items of clothing. No spatter of red blood standing stark against the green blades of grass in the beam of the torch's light.

At last, they were done, and still none the wiser.

Zoe and Shelley waited in the middle of the road as the search team from the other side of the street joined them with shaking heads and rounded shoulders, and they moved up to the other houses.

"They are outside of the range," Zoe said, chewing her lip.

"I know, but it's better to check," Shelley told her. "He was under stress. Maybe he made a mistake."

And so they woke the startled homeowners, and made them stand shivering in their pajamas on the cold lawn while they searched through every room for any sign of something abnormal. There was nothing in the attic. The house didn't even have a basement. No doors or windows had been forced, and no one had any relation whatsoever to the man they now knew was their killer.

There was no sign of her.

And when the other teams finished their searches without bringing up a single sign of Aisha Sparks either, Zoe knew that something was wrong.

"This does not make any sense," she said, slumping into the passenger seat again to rest. No matter how she thought about it, they had to have made the right calculations. The logarithm was not affected by human error. It had been correct about the last location. And they knew already that the man would never have deviated from the pattern, from the precise calculations they had used. He could not. It was not within his range of abilities to do so.

Beside her, Shelley climbed back behind the wheel, shifting on the seat to face her. "We have to think about it, Z," she said. "We're missing something. She isn't here yet."

"What was that? Say that again."

"She isn't here yet?"

Zoe nodded furiously, her mind whirring. "She does not have to be here yet. Not now." She checked the dashboard clock. "We still have six hours until dawn. She is not here now. But she will be tomorrow."

"How is that possible? The killer is dead. He can't bring anyone anywhere."

"Then there has to be some kind of outside force that we have not yet considered."

Shelley sunk her head into her hands in a momentary fit of despair, before raising bloodshot eyes again. "You sure the numbers are right?"

Zoe nodded once. "I have checked everything. We inputted the correct data, and the map stands up. A perfect Fibonacci spiral. There is nowhere else he could possibly go."

"All right." Shelley thought for a few minutes more, both of them aware of the unrelenting and callous tick on of the clock. "Maybe he has an accomplice. Someone who helped him get this far."

Zoe thought back. "But there was no evidence of another person at the crime scenes."

"There was barely any evidence of him at the crime scenes," Shelley pointed out. "What if this person stayed in the car every time? If their feet never touched the ground then they couldn't leave footprints. Maybe it's a woman, someone who would help him lure in his victims."

"He came in alone at the diner. A time when he needed a cover more than ever."

"Because she was already with the teenage girl, taking her away. Hiding her. Getting ready for tomorrow."

Zoe cocked her head. She had to admit, it held some water. "It would be peculiar for someone to maintain the same level of delusion. The apophenia. I have to admit, it would surprise me."

"Me, too," Shelley replied. "I don't like the idea of something coming out of left field at the last minute, something that we never saw coming, never had any clues about. But it's a possibility."

Zoe's mind was already moving forward, running toward other options. The idea of other people being involved opened doors. "Her family may be involved somehow," she said.

"Her family?"

"Maybe he threatens them. Forces them to report her missing so that we will be looking in all of the wrong places."

"I'm sure the troopers knew to check her house first," Shelley protested.

"Maybe not, if they already knew we were dealing with a serial killer." Zoe paused, chewing a fingernail. "He tells them they have to send Aisha out here at a certain time. They do not know that he is dead. They follow through."

"What threat could he possibly offer that would be a worse prospect than sending their daughter out alone and vulnerable?"

Zoe shrugged. She had no answer for that.

"It's a thought, anyway." Shelley opened the door again and swung out of the car, leaning back in to talk. "You sit here and rest. You shouldn't be running around like this. I'll talk to the troopers that interviewed her parents, and organize another search party for her house."

It was something. Then again, it could be nothing. Zoe sat back, closing her eyes against the patterns of lights and the low voices outside, trying to block everything out but the pattern. She had to concentrate. There had to be something else, an answer to this. Six hours, maybe less. Aisha waiting for rescue, maybe scared, maybe alone. The last person they could possibly save. If they didn't get this one, they would have lost them all.

Then Zoe thought about the expanse of grass beside the houses. The reason they had had to search empty ground, and not more buildings. This was the middle of a town; the developers would have built more housing there, unless they had a very specific reason not to.

And they had a reason not to. The train track that ran through the lower edge of the grass on the west side, the side that Zoe and Shelley had not personally searched. It ran at an angle to the road, cutting on through the land with the quickest possible route toward the nearest major town.

Tracks held trains, and trains held people. Trains moved people and things on a set schedule.

It was possible, in fact, to know when the first train would pass through any given area for the first time in a new day.

And she knew that she had him.

Zoe scrambled out of the car, nearly tripping over her seatbelt as it tangled in the ache of her arm and dangled below the edge of her seat. She jogged after Shelley, catching up with her as she left off talking to a cluster of troopers, all of whom were now turned away and talking on cells and radios.

"Train schedule," she said, the cold air biting off her words in a white cloud.

Shelley gave her a baffled look. "What?"

Zoe bit back exasperation. It wasn't Shelley's fault that she had not been inside Zoe's head, listening as she worked it all out. "I need the train schedule for those tracks. We need to know when the next trains will be coming through."

Zoe saw the moment that understanding flashed through Shelley's eyes, even in the gloom and contrast provided by the flashlights around them in the darkness. Shelley fumbled for her phone and searched up local contacts before making a call, stalking away from the group so that she could hear herself talk.

Zoe watched her grab a notebook from her pocket and lean it on the hood of their car, using the illumination from the interior light as she jotted down a series of notes. One, two, three, four—seven lines on the paper. Zoe crept closer, watching with bated breath until Shelley hung up the call and lifted the pad in the air.

"The first train passes through before dawn," Shelley said. "Four a.m., a freight train. They continue at half-hour intervals, until the single passenger train at a few minutes past seven a.m. I've ordered them to stop all trains leaving the rail yard and passenger depot, but we still need to find her."

Zoe thought it over. "Cross out the passenger train," she said. "It is too risky. There is no way he would be able to hide Aisha there, as well as some means of killing her. The trains are checked and cleaned before setting off in the morning. She would be found."

Shelley was looking something else up on her phone. "Sunrise is six fifty-two a.m. this morning."

Zoe looked up and shouted to the troopers who were standing, waiting for further instructions. "Check the tracks," she said. "Within our zone and for thirty feet in each direction. You are looking for wires, broken tracks, anything that might disrupt a train. Be careful. We may be dealing with explosives."

They broke and ran toward their new task, the urgency of the situation lost on no one. Lights danced across the road and grass, swaying up and down with the bobbing motion of a human run. They clustered like fireflies, then spread out as the troopers moved into a standard search formation, moving themselves at intervals across the area in question.

"What do you think?" Shelley asked. Her pendant glinted in the reflected light from Zoe's flashlight as she fidgeted, drawing it back and forth across the chain around her neck. "Would he wait for dawn? Or go for the first train?"

There were arguments to be made for each. Wait for an official new day to dawn, breaking the darkness and ensuring that no two kills were committed during the same period of darkness. Or go for the very first opportunity, ensuring that there was as little a chance as possible that Aisha would be found and saved in time.

They needed more data.

"Where do the trains originate from?" Zoe asked, a sudden thought striking her. "He had to have gone to the rail yard, snuck on board, set something up to keep Aisha in place at the very least, and then made it back to the diner."

"I'll make some calls," Shelley said, digging through her call list to find the last number she had dialed. "Hopefully the central rail yard can give me more information, or at least tell me who can."

Zoe watched the lights of the searchers at the tracks as Shelley spoke into the phone, all politeness but firm urgency. Her skin was crawling with the lack of action. It felt wrong, whiling away the hours of the night while the teen waited for them. She wanted to be running, digging, tearing up the ground around the tracks. Anything to ensure that there was nothing there, nothing that would disrupt the train's journey and send Aisha Sparks to her doom.

"Aha…yes, right…I see. Well, can you give me their number? Yes, I have a pen. All right…yes…"

The fireflies were moving further toward the edge of the area that Zoe had told them to search. Some of them had stopped moving entirely, having finished checking their area. It was not looking good.

"The good news is that I have the starting stations for each of the routes," Shelley said, putting her cell in front of her face as she copied another number from the notes she had written. "The bad news is that some of them will be held and loaded at an external freight yard, then moved to the starting station afterwards. Some were already loaded last night and moved to wait for the start of the day. I need to call someone else to track down which is which."

Zoe nodded absently, moving toward the searchers a few short steps at a time. She felt torn. Where was she better used? Over where the searchers already had their grids covered, or here, where only Shelley could make the calls?

If only she could think her way through this—figure out which train he would target by timing alone. It was not good enough just to stop them all, though Shelley had already done that. They still needed to figure out where Aisha was. They couldn't leave her there, locked inside a compartment somewhere, and hope that she would be spotted sooner or later. She had been away for over a day. God only knew what had been done to her.

"No answer," Shelley said, swearing quietly and moving her stiff, cold fingers over the screen again. "I'll try another. Middle of the damn night. No one is at their desks."

Zoe drifted away. "I will go help check the tracks," she said, having made up her mind that doing something was better than standing still.

She joined the grid of searchers, going back over ground that had already been checked in order to be extra thorough. Though the tracks themselves were uniform—each rail a set distance apart, with boards at set intervals between them, nuts and bolts and everything else laid out in predetermined pattern—their surroundings were anything but. Lumps of rock and tufts of grass, the tiny skeleton of a bird, items of trash that had blown across the empty land. It made searching harder work, trying to see an irregularity in a field of irregularities. So many patterns overlaid one over the other.

Forty minutes passed before Zoe was sure they had searched the tracks as thoroughly as they could. She looked up and saw Shelley sitting inside the car with the light on, still with her phone pressed to her ear. No luck there yet either, then.

Zoe paced, marking out distances with her feet as a way to distract herself. There was so much pent-up energy inside her, waiting to burst out. She wanted, needed, to *do* something. The troopers gathered in knots on the grass, all of them watched by the wary homeowners who stood now at their windows.

There was nothing on the tracks. Nothing that would have killed Aisha. So then, how would he do it?

The train. It had to be something on the train itself.

Zoe approached the car just in time to hear Shelley snap uncharacteristically, "Then wake him up!"

Shelley was pinching the bridge of her nose, a frown furrowing deep lines into her forehead. She took the cell from her ear and jabbed at the screen, ending yet another call.

"Nothing?" Zoe asked.

"I'm trying to get hold of the man who knows all the answers," Shelley said, shaking her head. "We've got to wait for someone to wake him up."

Zoe was about to comment on how ridiculous the whole situation was when Shelley's cell buzzed to life again, and Shelley grabbed it up.

"Hello? Yes, this is she...yes...and that's where?" Shelley made quick notes on her pad, scrawling out addresses next to the times. She showed them to Zoe, the locations of each of the trains that were due to head through the area.

Several were held in a rail yard a three-hour drive away, ready to depart soon in order to get here by their scheduled time. Only one was nearer—the first of the day, scheduled for around four in the morning when the rails began working again.

A twenty-minute drive, and just under three hours before it would leave the rail yard.

Zoe tapped the pad hurriedly, and Shelley started giving orders down the phone. "Is anyone there now? It's locked? Right, get us the person with the key. You have them? Excellent. Meet us there. Go in and start searching as soon as you arrive. We're looking for a teenage girl. But be cautious. Look through windows—don't open the car doors. We have reason to believe there may be traps in place."

"We are moving out," Zoe shouted, getting the attention of the troopers. "You six, stay here to man the roadblock and watch this area in case we do not find her. The rest of you, get in your cars and follow us."

CHAPTER TWENTY SEVEN

Zoe had already been strapped into her seat and was impatiently tapping her foot when Shelley ended the call. Their vehicle had roared into life, and they headed off down the road, their GPS calculating the fastest route and directing Shelley to turn at the end of the street with a robotic tone.

"I told him not to let the train depart," Shelley said. "It will never come through here."

"It does not matter," Zoe replied, clutching tightly to her seatbelt. "He set something up. She will die at the time that the train was scheduled to pass through here, even if it never leaves the rail yard. The tracks have not been tampered with, we know that now. There is something on the train itself."

Shelley's lips were a hard, thin line, pressed together so tightly that the edges were turning white. "I know," she said. "We'll have a little under two and a half hours to find her, figure out what the trap is, and get her out of it."

Zoe lifted her cell out of her pocket. "I will call for reinforcements. Bomb squad, and other specialists who will know more than we do."

The tires of the car ate the miles away, Shelley always keeping the speedometer over 100 no matter what type of road they turned onto. It was blissfully quiet, nearing half past one in the morning, the roads almost entirely empty. The one truck they did overtake at high speed blasted a horn at them, the sound trailing off into bemused silence as the two state police cars followed.

Zoe held onto her seatbelt and the door handle with white-knuckled fingers. Her stomach was roiling, but she would rather die than tell Shelley to slow down. Aisha's life depended on them getting there fast.

Shelley skidded to a stop at an entirely incorrect angle in the rail yard parking lot, and Zoe half-stumbled out of the door as she took a deep breath of fresh air to settle herself. She was a few steps behind as Shelley ran for the huge depot building, with massive openings where tracks allowed multiple trains in and out.

There was a five-foot-five man with wiry hair and a potbelly standing near an open entrance, a wad of papers in his hands that he was hurriedly leafing through. By the fact that he was wearing a winter jacket thrown on over what appeared to be pajamas, Zoe knew he was the man they had woken to come there.

"Smith?" Shelley shouted as they drew nearer.

He looked up in acknowledgment, then waved his papers. "I'm trying to identify the train. Says here that it should be in the sixth bay."

Zoe's eyes went up, taking in the scale of the place as they entered. Tracks and trains stretched into the distance. She counted nine bays across the front of the depot, and from this far corner she could see that they stretched back at least sixty cars deep. Multiple trains in each bay.

"Take us there," Shelley told him simply, and he turned and hurried along in front of them, still consulting the notes as he went.

The sixth bay was far enough away that precious minutes were gone, and then he had to double-check and cross-reference the plans before he was sure they were looking at the right engine.

"It's this one, all right," he said. "Freight service. Thirty-six boxcars. Each one is sealed with an individual door, but this is for cargo. Most of them don't have windows."

Zoe swore, looking down the length of the train. Thirty-six cars without windows. No way to see inside without endangering themselves.

"Which ones do?" Shelley asked.

"Eh, let's see...Driver car, sixth, sixteenth, and the last one."

Zoe turned to the troopers who had followed them in, panting with their run across the rail yard. "Go check those first. If you see something, report immediately."

They nodded and set off at a run again, each of them understanding fully that this was a matter of life and death. One trooper for each car. Somehow, they had managed to find the right ratio of people to bring.

Ratio—that made Zoe think. The cars with windows—that was significant, wasn't it? One, six, sixteen, thirty-six. A difference that doubled each time. Five, then ten, then twenty cars between them.

This was the correct train, all right.

"ETA on the specialists?" Zoe asked.

"Maybe thirty minutes, maybe a little more," Shelley said, holding onto the gold arrow pendant around her neck so hard that when she let go Zoe glimpsed the imprint on her palm. "I'll chase them up. And call an ambulance, in case we need them."

How long was it going to take them to search every car? When the specialists got here, they would have just a couple of hours to analyze and check the thirty-two that did not have windows. Two hours to be thorough enough that they could have confidence no agents or troopers would die on opening the door.

Not long enough.

Zoe racked her brains, pacing forward and back between their train and the one beside it. Her mind raced amongst the possibilities. She knew in her gut that the cars they were able to search now would not be the right ones. He wouldn't have made it so easy for them. He wouldn't have risked someone glancing through a window and seeing something that was not cargo at all.

There had to be something here that told him which car to pick. There was no way he would have chosen one at random—not their killer. Not an apophenic.

The central car? It seemed too obvious, and besides, with an even number of carriages there was no dead center. It would fall between two cars. There were thirty-six, so perhaps a multiple of six? But what did six mean to the killer? The number had not come up before. It wasn't in the Fibonacci sequence, and neither was thirty-six, for that matter. What was running through his head?

"Tell me everything you can about the train," Zoe said, turning on the depot manager again.

He stuttered for a moment, leafing through his papers. "Uh, well, it was manufactured in 2008," he said. "Came here in 2013."

Eight—thirteen. Those numbers caught on the edges of Zoe's mind, but she motioned for him to continue.

"Heavy-duty, heavy loads. It's rated for carrying some low-risk toxic materials. Takes between two and six journeys a day, based on load times and what it's booked for. Passes through an average of forty stations without stopping each journey, though sometimes deliveries can be more local or can even be split across different stations."

Zoe held up a hand to him to stop. He was just talking now, just meaningless noise. There were no numbers, no patterns in what he was saying. Averages held no weight. She needed the real data. Specifics.

But if the data was not in the system that was used to plan train schedules, then who would have had access to it? Certainly not a civilian. Not an outsider who had to pick a train despite not being an expert on them. There was something simpler here, some pattern that was visible from the outside. It would have caught the killer's eye.

Eight, thirteen—Zoe knew why they had stood out to her. They were numbers from the Fibonacci sequence. One, one, two, three, five, eight, thirteen, twenty-one, thirty-four...

Those numbers dictated the Fibonacci spiral's dimensions and points. And that was how many victims he had taken. Thirty-four, the man outside his farm. Twenty-one, the woman walking beside the road. Thirteen, the parking lot. Eight, Linda the gas station attendant. Five, Rubie in the woods. Three, the worker at the fair. Two, himself, lying in a pool of blood at the diner. And one, Aisha Sparks, trapped in the train car.

Taking the fact that the first and second point of the spiral were both the same number, and thus the same location, he would only have needed to kill there once. Meaning—what? The victim should be in the first car?

The trooper assigned to check there had already made a thorough search and moved on. There was nothing in the driver's cabin, and if the killer started his count from the first cargo car instead, he would have shortened that neat pattern of windowed cars. Ruined it, even, because the cabin had to count. The windows there could not be ignored.

The first car wasn't it. She had to think further, think past the sequence—

No. Not past it.

She just had to turn it upside down.

There was no time to explain.

She had to run.

Chapter Twenty Eight

The girl would be in the thirty-fourth carriage, to symbolize the completion of the spiral.

Shelley was yelling after her, but Zoe kept going at a headlong pace, rushing past a pair of stunned cops who were on their way down from their cars toward the rear of the train. They caught on and began to follow. Behind her, Zoe could count three pairs of footsteps and knew that everyone was on her tail. To the side the cars flashed by, counted so easily they may as well have had their numbers painted on the side.

Thirty-four cars was a long distance. Long enough that she had not quite been able to make out the right car from the front of the train, the rules of perspective slimming it down and hiding it from her perception. But now she was closer and she could see it, her goal. A car just like all of the others. No particular color or markings. But it was the one.

Zoe skidded to a stop, her heart thudding in her throat as she tried to catch her breath. Her eyes scanned every particular of the car from the side, searching for wires that did not belong, scrapes of missing paint, anything out of the ordinary. She hopped over connectors that were higher than her knees to check the other side, circling around it with determination.

"It's this one?" Shelley asked, breathlessly.

Zoe nodded sharply. "She's in here. It's the sequence."

Shelley seemed to understand that, even if she had been given no real explanation, and dropped to her knees to peer under the car. "I can't see anything suspicious."

The troopers had fanned out instinctively, rearranging themselves to all four points of the car, making their own kind of pattern. Zoe appreciated their efforts, but they were only hampering
her. There was nothing here that would be obvious. That was not
his style.

She approached the door of the car and banged on it, pressing her ear to the metal to listen for a response. "Aisha? Can you
hear me?"

There was nothing, even though she strained to hear it. She
held still for long seconds, barely even breathing, hoping to hear at
last a murmur of sound.

The girl was not conscious, whatever had been done to her. Zoe
pictured a razor-sharp wire tightening slowly and inexorably around
a sleeping girl's neck and shuddered, pushing away from the door.

But what was that? She leaned in again, taking another deep
inhalation through her nose. There was—something—some kind
of faint smell in the air…

Gas. It was gas.

"He is poisoning her air supply," Zoe gasped out, the second she
realized what it meant. "The car is filling with gas."

Shelley moved up next to her and pressed her own nose to the
hair-thin gap at the seal of the door, and nodded. "I smell it."

"We should wait for the other team to get here," one of the
troopers said nervously. "It could explode."

"Only if we introduce a spark," Zoe replied, shaking her head.
She could barely breathe, thinking of Aisha in there, the gas slowly
choking her lungs. "He was not an expert at using this kind of material, as far as we know. There is every possibility that he set it up
wrong. She could be dying even now."

"Or suffering irreparable damage, even if they do get her out
of there alive," Shelley agreed, tilting her head to turn wide eyes
sideways on Zoe. "What are you thinking?"

Zoe was not thinking at all. The decision had already been
made. It was the obvious one to make. "Everybody get back," she
said. "Way back. I am going to open the door."

"We should wait for the specialists," one of the troopers said.

"I am not waiting anymore," Zoe insisted. "Her life hangs in the balance. I outrank you. Go."

The troopers scuttled away without a further word of argument. They must have seen the determination in her face, and known that she would not take no for an answer.

"You, too," Zoe added, turning to Shelley. "Get behind cover. Just in case it does blow."

"I'm not leaving you. We started this together."

"You have a daughter." Zoe tried to keep her voice firm and level, but she was running out of patience. "Shelley, I need to open this door now. Go back with the others."

Shelley bit her lip and ducked her head. If there was light shining in her eyes when she looked up, it surely must have been a trick of the depot's overhead strips, and not gathering tears. "I'll stand here," she said. "Back you up."

Much as the troopers had been forced to cede under Zoe's determination, Zoe now found herself faced with Shelley's unwavering will. She could have argued, but the clock was ticking. "Stay by the side of the door. You will be protected from some of the blast. Be ready to move as soon as I come out."

Zoe took a steadying breath and waited for the sound of footsteps to recede into the distance. Then, raising her eyes to the ceiling in silent supplication to a God she was not sure existed, she set her hand on the door handle and twisted.

It came open easily, the electronic locks turned off with the train itself dormant. The sibilant hiss of gas leaking out into the air became apparent as soon as she stepped inside, waiting for her eyes to adjust to the gloom beyond the square of light afforded by the door.

Then she saw her.

Zoe leapt forward and touched her hands to Aisha Spark's neck, feeling a faint pulse beating under her fingertips with relief. In the far corner by the door the gas canister stood, marked with angry red symbols that told Zoe it would be better for her to get out as quickly as she could. It was big, enough that she could calculate a very dense concentration of it in the air of the car by the time it was emptied.

She approached it, searching for a valve or something that could be switched off. Her fingers encountered a small hole on the side of the tank, and the sound of the gas stopped as she pressed over it. A temporary solution at best. Casting around for something that would stick over it, Zoe felt herself already becoming a little light-headed and abandoned it. The gas tank could be dealt with by the professionals. She did not have the tools to plug the gap, and with that small of an opening, it would not yet have even emptied half out.

Zoe noted the presence of ropes at Aisha's ankles and wrists as she moved to lift the teenager into her arms. The girl weighed only one hundred and three pounds with her clothes, and was completely out cold, not even stirring as Zoe picked her up from the ground and stood.

She stepped outside, awkwardly maneuvering her load to swing the door shut with an elbow and contain the gas for now. Then she called out, her voice echoing across the lofty ceilings of the depot. "I have her! Where is that ambulance?"

EPILOGUE

Zoe took in gray skies and cool weather, not at all a surprise as they arrived home. The plane touched down with a rattle of the wheels, the passengers giving that little collective gasp of surprise and then relief that it bounced down onto the runway safely. Zoe left off looking out the window and started to gather her things, grabbing a notebook out of the pocket on the chair in front.

"Wait a moment," Shelley said beside her, stilling her with a gesture. She reached out and grasped one of Zoe's hands, facing her bodily. "I just wanted to say something."

Zoe tensed momentarily, but then relaxed. With anyone else, she would have been waiting for the speech: the one about how they weren't going to work as partners after this and should go their separate ways. But not from Shelley.

Zoe had long since stopped thinking of Shelley as a temporary inconvenience who would go away any day now. She had proven that she was in it for the long haul. Zoe had a feeling that their partnership was going to go very well indeed.

"No one is going to find out about your abilities, not from me," Shelley continued, squeezing Zoe's hand. "Not until you're ready, if that ever even happens. I'll keep your secret."

"Thank you," Zoe said, plain and simple. She might have faltered from time to time in polite conversation, but she knew the facts of this. She was grateful, deeply and sincerely. Shelley needed to know that. That was all that mattered.

And, for the first time, as she walked away from her partner at the airport, Zoe found herself actually looking forward to working with her again.

❧ ❧ ❧

Zoe came in through the door with a sigh of relief. A loud mewing from the kitchen, and the appearance of Euler with his tail held high in the air, told her that she was not the only one happy that she was home.

She dropped her overnight bag in the hall, promising herself that she would deal with it later. The first thing was to feed the cats, then herself, then shower. And possibly sleep for the next twenty-four hours.

After pouring out the cat food into bowls, Zoe scratched Pythagoras behind the ear until he batted her hand away with an impatient paw, eager to eat uninterrupted. She rested back on her heels, watching them for a moment.

Even if her cats only wanted her for her ability to provide food, at least she was not still persona non grata elsewhere. Far from being the failure her superiors had warned her against, Zoe's methods had been vindicated. Aisha Sparks had experienced mild symptoms from both the sedative she was given and the gas leak, but she had only needed to stay overnight in the hospital for observation. She had been discharged before Shelley and Zoe had finished tying up loose ends and gotten themselves back on a plane.

With the evidence that the killer really had targeted the fair, and it was only the forensic mistake of assuming the color of his car that got in the way, it was now clear to everyone that Zoe had been on the right path. The latest call from the Chief had been quite the opposite from the last—high praise and congratulations. She was being described as a brilliant agent with deductive powers beyond that of the norm in internal conversations, and the press was already having a field day with the killer's mental problems. The rumors would go away, as would the praise. There was always another case.

But something had been different this time. Something had changed inside her, something seismic. She had never before compared herself directly to a serial killer, found so many things in common. Zoe had emerged from that stronger, her own belief in herself having survived the storm. She was a good person. Even her mother's voice still screaming in the back of her head could not change that.

Part of the victory she felt must surely have come from the other first of this case: the first agent to figure out her abilities and not run a mile. Others had never even asked about them. They just got spooked and walked away, unable to deal with Zoe's idiosyncrasies and the fact that she was always the quickest to solve the case. Shelley was different. Zoe could feel already the difference it made. The confidence that had grown in her.

Maybe if she'd confided in Shelley sooner, Zoe would have been able to stop the pattern earlier and save more lives. That was her one regret.

She left the cats alone and stood, sifting through her freezer to pull out something easy to shove in the oven. She winced at the pull in her arm as she extended it slightly too far, feeling the catch of her new stitches. That was going to take some getting used to. The doctor had warned her that she might be in line for a nasty scar, given the amount of time she had left before getting it seen to.

Zoe made her way over to the familiar frame of her computer, firing it up. At least typing was not going to put any particular strain on the wound. As her dinner cooked, she logged into her email account, checking for updates.

There was a message, actually, buried under the ten junk emails and the usual official requests that she report for Bureau counseling after having fired her weapon. It was not one that she had expected. The property lawyer, John, who had sat through that uncomfortable date what now felt like months ago, filled up on the breadbasket, and wished her well at the end of the night with no promise of a follow-up. She had not expected to hear from him ever again, in fact, yet there was his name, thrown up by the same dating site he had contacted her through in the first place.

Hi Zoe, hope you're well. I keep thinking about our date. I was a bit dull, distracted by a case if I'm honest. Will you give me a second chance?

Zoe thought it over, one ear listening for the ding of the oven timer as she examined his message several times. How strange. There she thought that she had been the one to mess up the date, and he was thinking the same thing. Maybe they were both fifty percent to blame. She would even take ninety-eight, because that was better than one hundred.

The ten-point font blinked at her until she turned with determination and picked up her cell and dialed a number. It rang four times before the line crackled into a clearer sound.

"Hello?"

Zoe blinked. She had almost not expected an answer. "Hello, is this Dr. Lauren Monk?"

"Yes, speaking. How can I help?"

Zoe steeled herself. It really was time to make the leap. She was nowhere near ready to try going on a second date with a guy, least of all one who might actually have presented an interesting prospect. She needed to work on herself, and the demons that still kept her awake at night, if she was going to move forward in any meaningful way.

And now that she had a permanent partner, it would probably be good for Shelley's sake if she could learn to be a little bit less prickly, too.

"I was referred to you by Dr. Applewhite. My name is Zoe Prime. I would like to make an appointment."

As she made a note of the date in her diary, she just hoped that she would not be called out of state on another case before she had a chance to keep it.